Body on the Bayou

by

Cynthia Harrison

Body on the Bayou

Cover Art by *Diana Carlile*

The Wild Rose Press, Inc.
PO Box 708
Adams Basin, NY 14410-0708
Visit us at www.thewildrosepress.com

Publishing History
First Edition, 2023
Trade Paperback ISBN 978-1-5092-5156-8
Digital ISBN 978-1-5092-5157-5

Published in the United States of America

Dedication

To Sisters in Crime, especially my critique group and our fearless leader Jan Rydzon.

Chapter One

"It's a fake," Jane Chasen said as she absorbed the form and color of the framed artwork. She hated to be so blunt, even to a bitch like Marva, so she added, "But a very good one." It was true. This was a reproduction. The artist, probably someone who did reproductions for a living, had left their unmistakable mark.

"What?" screeched Marva, the neighborhood diva. "Oh, what do you know, anyway?" Marva's face turned several shades of purple.

Jane's stomach flipped. She rarely had to deal with people who'd been ripped off. Or maybe Marva was lying. Marva could have bought this fake knowing it was a reproduction and then tried to fool a few select neighbors. But she'd been wrong to think she could fool Jane, an art expert who had worked with the St. Pete PD as a consultant on the art aspects of a murder case just a month ago.

Marva pinned Jane with her evil eye and then hung her head and moaned softly. Maybe Marva didn't know it was a fake. Maybe her husband had gifted it to her and lied about it. Jane waited until Marva composed herself. The stages of grief in art forgery paralleled how humans dealt with death. First, disbelief. Then anger. Finally, most of the time, a numb acceptance. Or, in rare cases, a strong need for revenge.

"Get out," Marva said, pointing a long bloodred

fingernail at the door in her massive foyer.

There went hope.

Jane shrugged and stepped toward the door. She'd been too abrupt, although there was never a good way to tell someone they'd been duped. But Marva was rude, bitchy, arrogant, and, worst of all in Jane's view, ignorant about art. There were not enough Frida Kahlo originals out there for an owner at Winding Bayou, even a penthouse owner, to have purchased one. The last original self-portrait to sell went for thirty-five million at a Sotheby's auction in 2021.

"No. Wait! What makes you think it's a fake?"

Last night, after the Frida exhibit viewing, the ladies had dinner downtown at a sleek, retro surf-and-turf place on Tampa Bay. Everyone talked not about the artist but Marva's fabulous art collection, her massive condo, her world travels. This bothered Jane. She'd looked forward to discussing Kahlo. She was seated beside Marva at dinner and, trying for delicacy, switched the topic to the exhibit of Kahlo's memorabilia and work.

"Frida wasn't well known in her lifetime. She was more an artist's artist. The French Surrealists were crazy about her, but she wasn't famous like her husband."

"Diego Rivera," Queenie said. "Mexican muralist and painter."

"Yeah, there was a photo of the two of them in the exhibit. Her so tiny and him so huge," Marva said.

"She gave away or sold most of her early work. Painted her first self-portrait as a way to woo back a reluctant lover. This was before she married Diego."

"I fail to see why she'd give herself such awful eyebrows," Marva remarked. A few of the women tittered. "You could tell from the photos that they weren't as bad, er, as bold, as she painted them."

"Just the point," Jane said, glancing down the table at her friends Barb and Kim, who were probably having a way more fun conversation. Bubbles of their laughter floated down the table. Ah, well. Here she was at the top of the table, and she'd make the best of it. Jane had retired from art lecturing a few years ago and didn't relish going into that mode. But sometimes she felt like she was in the world not just to be a new granny, which she loved more than art, but to keep certain facts straight regarding favorite artists. "The brows are painted to resemble the wings of a blackbird. They draw attention to her eyes. They mesmerize."

Marva whispered to Jane that she'd recently acquired a Kahlo on a visit to Taos, New Mexico.

Why whisper? Was this confidential? Surely, they didn't have a secret billionaire living at the Bayou, even if she owned the penthouse.

"Come on up tomorrow and I'll show it to you." She still whispered. Weird and rude.

"Well?" Marva said, bringing Jane back to the present. To the penthouse.

Jane did her best to soften the blow. "It's very nicely done. Quite in her late style, those in the diary. You've read it?"

"No, I don't know what diary you're talking about." Marva sniffed and scratched her nose with her long pointy nail. "Or what it has to do with this watercolor. It was a gift from Frida to Georgia O'Keefe. I snapped it up when I spotted it in a Taos gallery."

There went the theory Marva's husband had told her it was an original. Jane didn't ask her how much she'd paid for the painting. Instead, she searched for tactful phrasing.

"You're right, Frida and Georgia were friends," Jane said, not adding that they were likely lovers for a time, too. "And Frida's *Self Portrait on the Borderline* was painted as a homage to Georgia."

Marva crossed her arms. "Yeah, yeah, but she could have very well done a personal smaller picture like mine and sent it to Georgia. You see she signed it!" Marva's fingernail pointed out the signature line.

"I believe this piece you have is a near copy of a 1953 work. For the last ten years of her life, Frida kept out of the public eye. She still painted, but she did it in private. She drew and did the watercolors in a different style using a diary. She did not share this diary with anyone. In it, she included sketches and watercolor paintings in this style, more muted than the precise oil self-portraits we know so well. One layer in some of the little watercolors depicts two women, but, then again, this is the woman who painted *The Two Fridas*. When Frida died, the diary was put away for a decade. It was only recently discovered, long after O'Keefe's death in 1985. There was no way Frida gave the diary to O'Keefe. She hadn't shown it to anyone. It remained unknown, tucked away for years."

"I don't believe you. That is Kahlo's signature."

Jane's gaze swept over the wall crowded with framed art before studying the stylized F and the date. In the diary, there was a flourished F just like this one. She didn't want to debate signatures. She didn't want to ask if Marva had had it appraised or insured. She just had to give the one fact that clarified why she was so sure this was not a Kahlo, but a clever fake.

"She often dated her work and did so in the diary. If

you notice, your watercolor is dated 1955. Frida died in 1954."

Jane didn't look at Marva. Instead, her gaze fixed on the Matisse, in a place of honor with its own spotlight, undoubtedly another forgery. Marva may live in the penthouse as large as an entire floor of condos in Winding Bayou, but the original of this particular Matisse hung in a Chicago museum. She decided to pick her battles and did not mention the Matisse to Marva.

Before Marva could respond, a man as large as Diego himself banged into the foyer, slamming the door.

"Ray!" Marva said. She looked from the man to Jane, momentarily speechless. Her face flared with splotches, and her eyes implored Jane not to mention anything about the Kahlo.

Jane, distracted by Ray's overwhelming scent of expensive musky cologne, figured the odd note must be Florida sweat.

"Jane, this is my husband, Ray. Ray, our neighbor, Jane."

"Don't you mean ex-husband?" Ray said, his voice dismissive. He didn't bother to acknowledge Jane. "I just came back for some clothes." He stalked down the hall, taking his smell with him.

"We're not exactly divorced yet," Marva said in a low voice. "But he said I can keep the penthouse and the art. He's the one who bought me the Matisse. Excuse me a minute." Marva rushed after Ray.

Jane looked around the wide, large room Marva called the salon. Two groupings of teal-and-white-striped sofas and gold tufted chairs were at the far end, which led into a hallway directly opposite the hallway Ray had stomped down. Classic main hall with two wing design. Jane wanted to leave but must at least say good-bye to Marva before she did. She surveyed her surroundings a bit more closely.

A huge tobacco-brown recliner faced a large television on the wall across from the art wall, as Marva called it. The chair and television begged for a room of their own. Surely they had space for it. In the middle of the room, dividing the rest of the furniture groupings, a lovely large, fluted bowl sat atop a reproduction piecrust table. Sad mistake. The flutes of the bowl clashed with the scallops of the piecrust table. Chihuly, Jane thought of the bowl, chosen to match the white-and-teal color scheme of the room. Then she looked again. St. Pete had a small Chihuly museum with a gift shop attached. A bowl like this might sell for a couple thousand dollars if original, but if a student's work, far less. Just on the basis of the art wall reproductions, Jane pegged the bowl as a gifted student's work.

Jane moved across the room to inspect the piece. The glass, at least, was authentic. Jane knew Chihuly's lush colors well. Her daughter lived in Seattle, where Chihuly worked in an old warehouse near the docks. The much larger museum devoted to his work was across town near the Space Needle. Jane had visited both museums many times, most recently with her daughter and granddaughter just six months after Suzy's birth. She missed her. But two more grandchildren were on the way, and that made her happy.

She stood viewing the art wall from a bit farther away. She recognized some newer St. Pete painters among the works—Hart Love, Olivia Solten, the guy who did the interesting street scenes, what was his name? Getting old unnerved Jane. She was thinking the room wanted more space between the various works when Marva rushed down the hall.

Jane bit her lip. "I should go."

"No, please, stay until he leaves," Marva whispered, grasping Jane's hand and tugging.

One thing Jane had discovered over last night's after-museum dinner was that she and Marva did have one thing in common, an enthusiastic appreciation for buttery Chardonnay. There were no clocks anywhere, but she'd come up at noon; surely one glass wouldn't hurt. And Marva had almost begged. So, she let Marva lead her into the kitchen where Jane's vision was stunned by sparkling teal appliances. Too much. She looked toward the triple glass slider leading out to a lanai and the open-air garden beyond it. The colors of nature calmed her overstimulated eyes.

"I love your lanai," Jane said. A young woman in jean shorts and a white sleeveless top fussed with the raised plantings.

"My assistant, Abigail," Marva said. "Don't mind her." She poured chilled wine almost to the top of two crystal wineglasses. White wine in red wine glasses, but that was fine. Red wine glasses were larger. "Cheers," Marva said.

They sat at the counter where, Jane surmised, Marva could see the hallway. She hadn't had more than a few sips of wine before Ray rolled out two large black suitcases.

"Ray!" Marva said, standing. "I want my keys."

He left one bag standing on its wheels while he fished in his pants pocket for the keys. He set them into her palm with what looked like a wicked poke, resumed his grip on the case, and left the penthouse, slamming the door behind him.

Marva threw the keys and a plastic card the size of a driver's license onto her white-and-gold kitchen counter, which was sumptuous, made of hard, sparkly, shiny stone. Like so much of Marva's home, it screamed money if not exactly exquisite taste.

Jane took a large sip of wine. She wanted out of there almost as much as Ray.

"He's probably made another set. I have a locksmith coming to change the locks. Won't he be surprised next time he tries to march in here unannounced?"

"Why wouldn't he be able to buzz up the elevator?" Everyone in the building knew elevator access to the penthouse was limited to its owners.

Marva picked up the card. "This is his key card for the elevator. I don't think he can get another one. I'll have to call the office."

"I'm so sorry things didn't work out."

"Don't be. I'm not. Let the bastard move in with Biffy." Marva poured herself another brimming glass of Chardonnay. She held the nearly depleted bottle up, looking toward Jane.

Jane shook her head. "I've really got to get going."

Assistant Abigail had disappeared. Jane heard movement somewhere in the house. There must be more sliders in at least one of the many, many rooms onto the lanai besides these in the kitchen. Maybe Abigail had an office? Jane would never know. She didn't plan to get chummy with Marva.

Chapter Two

Jane strolled to the pool an hour before cocktail time so she could visit with Barb and George, her married neighbors and good friends. Barb did not do cocktail hour these days; she was pregnant, a rare sight in Winding Bayou. She followed a strict regime, which seemed not to box her in at all. Barb had been in the FBI when Jane met her. She was now a private investigator working for a group of flashy attorneys. George had at one time been her CI. He was now consulting on a true-crime story about that period of his life.

Jane settled herself at the edge of the pool, feet dangling in the water. She let life flow back to normal. Every day was beautiful and odd. In Florida, colors were brighter, and energy buzzed through the air like invisible hummingbirds.

George and Barb joined her at the pool, Barb only dipping her toes in. George jumped in with a cannonball that splashed both his wife, who laughed, and Grant, the property manager, who did not. Grant had been yelling at Fred, his second-in-command. Fred had not been fired last month despite being an unwitting accomplice to murder. Instead, the owners had hired property manager Grant who seemed to live in his office beside the pool, which had been converted from last-century cabanas. He never seemed to inspect so much as a blade of grass. He did have a nice tan, though.

Jane's high spirits bobbled a bit, when Grant, whose grey uniform had only got a little wet when he'd been cannonballed, turned to George, the only person in the pool, and growled, "Knock it off, hot shot."

Jane and Barb looked at each other.

"You know him?" Barb asked.

"Grant, Fred's babysitter," Jane whispered.

Fred's babysitter was a masterful pain.

"Why is he being so rude to George?"

Jane didn't know Grant well, but what she knew, she did not like. She texted Kim, who was not at the pool yet.

Kim texted back. —*Hot head. Nobody likes him. Poor Fred.*—

Jane showed Kim's text to Barb.

"So, Fred is on probation. I wondered why they'd kept him on." There was still a lot of FBI left in Barb.

In Jane's opinion, Fred could not help getting caught up in the murder scheme. He didn't know anything and had been used as a handy tool. Grant had been Fred's punishment, along with demotion and humiliation.

"At least Fred's a nice guy," Barb said.

Jane agreed. She wished Grant would go back to the grass where he slithered from, the hissing snake.

George exchanged increasingly heated words with Grant, who loomed large over George in the pool.

"I'm in charge, and if you don't watch out, you'll be banned from the pool," Grant said.

"Ha. You can't ban residents. Pool access is in my condo agreement. I own a piece of this pool, and you're just a pool boy I pay to keep it clean." George smacked the water with his hand before hoisting himself out of of the pool.

"Listen, dumbass, I have complete authority!" Grant

said, oblivious to George's gym-rat muscles shiny with water.

Jane and Barb jumped up and hastened over to the shouting match.

"George," Jane asked. "How's the screenplay going?"

Barb folded her arms against her stomach and glared at Grant, who whirled around and stalked toward the shower rooms. He was tall and thin, and Jane pictured George breaking him in two like a cookie.

"Who is that asshole?" George said loud enough for Grant to hear as he stalked toward the shower rooms. Then he said, "Never mind," and answered Jane's original question about his beloved screenplay, the true-crime story of his involvement with a Detroit mob, turning informant for the FBI, testifying at several trials, ending with him lying low in Florida, holed up in Winding Bayou. When one of the Detroit mob escaped from a low-security prison and came after George, he reluctantly became Barb's informant again, because he loved her. In the third act, the FBI agent and CI marry. Happily ever after, or at least for now. How could Hollywood resist it?

"Oh, you know, we talk every day, the writers ask me questions." He shrugged. "It's a living." Also a thinly veiled true story of George's transition from a petty criminal to government informer to family man. "They're talking about locations now."

"Will they start in Detroit?" Jane asked. Both Jane and George had moved to St. Pete from Detroit at about the same time not even a year ago and became neighbors in the mostly retiree Winding Bayou community. It seemed everyone was from Michigan, New York, or

Canada.

"Yeah. They actually got permission to use my shitty flat in Mexicantown."

Jane's heart accelerated. "Won't that"—she searched for the word—"compromise your security?"

"Naw. Donaldsin's the new snitch. I'm history."

Donaldsin was the guy the mob sent to Florida last month to take out George. Instead, Barb put him behind bars for life.

Barb, infinitely patient, said, "What do we have to do to file a complaint about that asshole who yelled at you for getting a few drops of water on his geezer uniform shorts and shirt?"

"We let it be and go home," George said.

"Good! Get the hell out of here," Grant yelled from the vicinity of his cabana. "No kids allowed in the pool at cocktail hour!"

George flipped him off.

Grant pretended not to see.

The ladies gathering for drinks ignored the squabble. Jane's artist friend, Queenie, strolled into the pool area wearing a turquoise caftan. She toted a jug of something tropical and no doubt alcoholic. Beth and Hazel, right behind Queenie, carried delicious trays of snacks. Jane hugged Kim, her first friend in Winding Bayou, careful not to break any bones of the tiny petite blonde.

"Pull up a seat," Kim said. "Queenie made her famous sangria."

Lethal was more like it. To the wine and fruit, Queenie added "just a smidge" of a liqueur made in St. Pete from Florida oranges. Lovely stuff. And Jane was thirsty from sitting in the sun. The group had commandeered an umbrella table by the pool. Jane grabbed the last chair.

One drink wouldn't hurt. "Hey, ladies. I'm just staying for one. I've been out in the sun for an hour already."

Queenie poured Jane a cocktail.

"See you, Jane! Ladies!" George called, as he and Barb departed the pool area.

Barb yelled, "Y'all don't get too rowdy, now."

Jane waved.

"Cute kids, but I cannot for the life of me figure out why a young couple wants to live with us old folks," Hazel said.

"Speak for yourself," said Kim, sipping her cocktail. "Age is just a number."

The ladies piled crab salad on cucumber coins and added shrimp from a heaping tray to their plates. Kim produced a bowl of marcona almonds from her beach bag, passing it around.

"I hear they're allowing up to twenty percent of owners to be under age fifty-five."

"That's a shame," Hazel said.

Her husband was known for his roving eyes that always fastened themselves on women's breasts, never their faces. Jane knew because he did it to her every time she saw him. He even ogled people's teenaged granddaughters when they came for spring-break visits. There were rumors he had a telescope in the second bedroom of the condo. Hazel said he liked stargazing, but she had to know better.

"So, did you hear Marva's moving?" Queenie said.

Jane was stunned. Marva hadn't said a word to her about it. In fact, she'd said her husband was giving her the penthouse in the divorce. But she kept quiet. Maybe later, when they were alone, she'd tell Kim about her visit to Marva's earlier today, her discovery of the dubious paintings, and meeting Marva's brutish almost-ex. But none of that was gossip for cocktail time at the pool. At first meeting, and even earlier today, Jane had disliked Marva, but she pitied her, too. Why was she moving? What had changed? "Is the condo on the market?" Jane asked.

"Yep! Premarket, they call it," Queenie said. "She's looking for a place in Arizona, or she may stay in Florida, across the bridge."

The Sunshine Skyway, a long, tall suspension bridge, spanned Tampa Bay. It had been built after the first bridge collapsed during rush-hour traffic. Thirty-seven souls sank to watery graves that day. The remains of the first bridge were visible as you drove over the new one. People fished off the now-tourist site, but both bridges made Jane shudder. She tried not to go south of St. Pete, the last city before the bridge that led to Bradenton, Sarasota, and down to Naples. Jane took a sip of the strong sangria, eyeing the crab salad.

"That was sad about Big Snapper," someone said, changing the subject. Big Snapper had been the Bayou's resident gator for many years until he'd gotten too large for their little bayou and had to be carted off to the Everglades.

"There's still Mama Snapper and two babies."

"Those babies got so big!" Phones with baby gator pics circulated. Then the grandchildren. Jane passed around the latest of Suzy, in a yellow dress, smiling big, holding herself upright with the help of a shiny yellow sports car.

"I hope Mama and her children don't sun on the lawn by the pool, the way Big Snapper did," Jane said.

Everyone laughed. Jane blushed. It was no secret that she was fearful of gators. Also geckos. She'd called Kim in a panic when a gecko got into her condo, and Kim had simply come up with a shoebox and newspaper, collected the harmless reptile, and released him outdoors. Likewise, gators didn't bother humans unless they felt attacked or the person appeared to be a fish. One foolish snowbird, sitting on an old broken dock off the bayou, had dangled her brightly painted toes in the water, not bothering to push aside the tall grasses that grew along the shore. Sure enough, Big Snapper thought the foot was a fish, and he went for it. The woman was fine. Her husband had punched Snap in the nose, and he let go. Still, that was probably the real reason Big Snapper had been removed from their bayou.

"Marva's got family down Alligator Alley," Queenie said. "Not that she'd ever admit to growing up in Everglades City. But she's got a sister there and a nephew. She can lord her money over them if she buys a mansion in Naples."

Jane scooped crab onto a cucumber slice. It was delicious, and she was hungry. She could make a meal out of these little snacks.

"No kids?" one of the ladies asked about Marva.

Jane was determined not to say a thing about meeting Marva's almost-ex and seeing her gallery wall. She for sure didn't want to mention the forgeries/reproductions. She was almost sorry she'd seen them.

"No, they never had any." Hazel knew Marva best. "But her soon-to-be ex is about to marry a person called

Biffy who has a kid by her first husband."

"Is it true Marva's husband is into threesomes?"

Hazel sniffed. "He has affairs. Like with the help. Or bimbos he picks up in bars."

Jane's head floated on her shoulders. She'd finished that glass of punch too fast. And on an empty stomach. "Ladies, it was so nice to see you all, but I have got to get home."

"Not staying for one more glass of punch?" Kim said. "There's plenty."

"I've got a date with Jesse tonight, so I better not," Jane said. "Also, I can't feel my lips." She poked at her mouth, messing up her lipstick, some of which landed on her teeth.

Kim pointed this out.

Jane shrugged and scrubbed her teeth with a finger. "Delicious but lethal, Queenie."

Everyone laughed. Jane waved at her neighbors and friends as she rose to try her luck at walking a straight line home. More people had gathered around the umbrella tables and set up their mini bars. The nightly poolside cocktail party was in full swing.

****

Jane walked the short way to her building, thinking about how lovely it would be to see Jesse again. Her tummy fizzed, and her skin prickled in anticipation. He was almost too good at his job, but Jane respected that about him, because as a police detective, he went into immediate action. He'd postponed their last date when he spotted a very old woman, dazed look on her face, dancing down Central Avenue in a bathrobe. It took some time, but he'd found the dementia facility where she lived. Then he located her next of kin. That was

Jesse, kind, compassionate, and good at his job.

As her thoughts ribboned out in an untidy spool, she almost walked right into a woman who tried to get around her on the skinny sidewalk path.

"Oh!" Jane said. They both stopped. "You're Abigail, Marva's assistant."

Abigail gave Jane a strange look.

"Ha, that's right. You were out watering the plants when I was over earlier today. I'm Jane."

Abigail smiled. "You sure pissed off my boss."

"Truth hurts." Jane gathered Abigail, like many other Winding Bayou folk, wasn't overly fond of Marva, because the young woman giggled.

Chapter Three

Jane climbed the stairs to her second-floor condo, beyond excited to see Jesse this evening. Their romance had started a few months ago, and he'd stayed overnight at hers on Thanksgiving, just after they'd solved the case of a murdered artist. They'd progressed to his keeping a clean set of clothes and a razor at her place, which considering Jane's nonexistent love life before Jesse, including most of her married years, was way more than nice.

A text buzzed, and Jane looked at her phone. Her friend Patrice. Also Jesse's detective partner. Patrice's husband had left her with three kids, and she pleaded with Jane to understand why she had no time for dinner and drinks these days. —*My parents moved in—I've got the midnight shift. It's a nightmare. But it could be so much worse.*—

—*Not a problem.*— Jane typed back. —*We'll get together when things settle down xo.*—

Jane clicked her phone off and wondered if divorce came in threes. Patrice, Marva…who next?

She opened her closet to search for something delicious to wear. She had a few pretty dresses that she'd not worn for ages. She chose a floaty coral number that matched her new manicure. She finger-combed her silver hair into damp waves after a long soak in the tub. She'd just sprayed on Jesse's favorite perfume when the bell rang. Jane opened the door to her favorite man in the world.

"Hey, Shug," Jesse said, taking her in his arms.

He moved them into the hall, kicking the door shut before he kissed her, walking her slowly back into the bedroom.

All of life dissolved into a kiss soft as a cloud. Which led to other endeavors. Jane's dress, a wrinkled heap on the floor, was no longer fit to be worn, and anyway, they'd missed their dinner reservation. Both were starving, so they ordered meatballs and a baguette from Two to Go and stopped for wine at the enormous liquor store on Tyrone. Then they went back to Jane's place to eat.

After dinner, Jesse didn't even sit on his recliner but shared the sofa with Jane.

She laid her head on his shoulder. "I missed you."

"I missed you, too." He hugged both his arms around her.

They'd seen each other two days ago.

"Patrice's husband left her," Jesse said.

"I know." So much for romantic cuddles. Jane didn't know much about Patrice's marriage. Just that they'd been young and had kids right away.

"He thinks he can do better," Jesse said.

"You're kidding?" Patrice was gorgeous and tough, also the main breadwinner in her family.

"Nope. He doesn't like being married to a police detective."

"But a beat cop was okay? What a jerk. Here she was, looking out for her kids and him, Mr. House Husband, and he dumps her."

"Yeah. She got the house, though. Her folks moved

in to help with the kids, and everything's okay, I think. She's not been super communicative lately," Jesse said.

"She only has time to text me. But I didn't know she's working midnights?"

"Someone's on vacation. She'll be back with me Monday."

"Be extra nice to her. She's having a hard time," Jane said. She had a feeling there was more to the story than Patrice was telling her.

After dinner, Jane and Jesse tackled the dishes together. Jesse washed and Jane dried. As he handed her a plate, she casually said, "Jesse, are you staying over?

"If that's okay," he said, polishing the last wine glass himself.

"Sure. I was hoping you would," Jane said, satisfied.

Chapter Four

Hazel Pentress woke up at four a.m. and reached across her king-sized bed. Ethan was not next to her. Was he in his observation room? Instead of getting up to check on him, she fretted. Ethan had been an astronomy buff their entire married life of forty-one years. But Hazel sometimes caught him looking at the pool through his telescope lens. Or the girls in the pool. She wasn't as stupid as her friends thought she was.

Ethan got fixated on things. He'd been into astronomy since college, then taught it at the community college where they met. She blamed the new interest in women's breasts, all shapes and sizes, on Ray, Ethan's only friend since they'd moved. It was a tic or a quirk or something, but it was also embarrassing as hell. Hazel had even caught him sizing up his own pectoral muscles. He joined a gym with the idea that he'd build them up but lost interest pretty quickly. Although he was still interested in man boobs. Other men's boobs, the ones with a B or C cup. They'd gone for counselling about it back when the obsessive behavior started. Mostly it had helped Hazel understand that with Ethan, boobs were not a sexual thing. They might as well be stars.

He came back in the room about six a.m. and slid in beside her. They had a blackout blind, so if not for the clock telling a different story, it could be midnight.

"Where were you? Observation room?" That's what

he called the small guest bedroom with the large telescope.

"No." Ethan cuddled up into his side sleep position. Knees bent and one hand under his pillow.

"Ethan!"

"What? It's early, Hazel. Let's try to sleep."

"I worried when you weren't in bed."

"No need."

"Ethan, where were you?" Hazel knew her husband was both brilliant and socially awkward. He didn't talk much to strangers, although he talked to her. She had to force him to be friends with Ray, the husband of her best friend, Marva. All that did was give Ethan a dark twisty concept of how a man should act. Drinking and checking out women's bodies.

He sighed and turned to lie on his back. "Watching Eta Aquarido."

Hazel relaxed. "Anything good?"

"Oh yes."

Eta Aquarido was cosmic dust, a meteor shower, from the ancient Halley comet. People had been observing Eta A since ancient times. Hazel knew about all the various night events. When she was younger, she'd even sometimes watch them with Ethan. Back when the kids were young, they'd had a cottage and she and Ethan would slip out to the boat, putter to the middle of the lake, and lie back to watch the show in the sky. But that had been in Wisconsin. This was Florida, where shrubbery grew as tall as trees. The only place Ethan could get a big enough patch of sky was at the picnic area across the boulevard where he could stretch out on a table next to the barbecue. He had a special quilted space blanket he spread on the table and laid himself out, much as he was doing now, stargazing. For meteor showers, he didn't need his telescope or even binoculars. The best way to see them was to latch onto a big piece of sky and scan it.

Beside her, Ethan snored.

She wouldn't sleep anymore. She got up and put a pot of coffee on.

Chapter Five

Jane and Jesse sipped coffee in the sunroom. Jesse liked to hike around the bayou early, before it got too hot, although in early December, the temperatures were beginning to inch cooler, the soothing tap of summer rain on the roof long gone. They were already laced up and Jesse was ready to rock, but Jane needed coffee first. Nice of Jesse to indulge her.

Jesse, always one to take the lead, walked slightly ahead of Jane, following the path to the trail behind Jane's building. They started off at a good pace, birds squawking as they rose from the bushes, small animals scuttling away. They were at about the halfway point when they found the body, nude from the waist up. A long sheer skirt, the color of seaweed, was carefully placed around the torso and legs. The hair. The face. Jane had a hard time believing what she was seeing.

"Jesse! That's my neighbor, Marva. God, I just saw her yesterday."

Jesse had his pad of paper out, searched fruitlessly for a pencil.

"Did you bring your phone?" Jane asked.

"Yeah, sure."

"Use your notebook function." Jesse fumbled with his paper notebook, put it in his pocket, and stared at his phone for a beat.

"Here," Jane said. "Press that app."

The notebook came up.

"Now type in your notes."

"Okay. Unless you want to help."

Jane's hands trembled so bad she wasn't sure she could work a small keyboard. She was starting to smell the body. How long had it been here? Why weren't the vultures circling overhead swooping down? "I'll call Patrice," she said.

Jesse pecked at the notebook. Then as she explained to Patrice what was going on, Jesse snapped a few photos of the body from different angles.

They were on the other side of the bayou from the four condo buildings that made up the Winding Bayou complex. Jesse officially called in the death, because Marva was very obviously dead, and they waited there until police and crime scene people started to show up. Patrice was first on scene, and she automatically handed Jesse a pencil.

"I'm using the notepad on my phone now." He smirked.

"Welcome to the twenty-first century," she retorted.

Jane wondered how they could joke with a dead woman in front of them.

"Do you know Marva's last name?" Jesse asked Jane, his fingers hovering over the tiny keyboard of his phone.

"Battington."

"Married? Kids?"

Jane averted her eyes from the body. It had been positioned in a precise way, even her arms, gathering ants now, had been styled. And she was on her back, looking at the sky.

"Jane."

Jesse had asked her something about the case, but her ears were full of insect buzzing. She could not hear him.

He repeated his question, louder now.

"No kids. Married, but separated. I saw him too yesterday, but I can't remember his name. He came to pack some clothes while I was there. Big guy." Intimidating, she thought but didn't say. "Marva seemed a little afraid of him. I wanted to leave when he got there, but she almost begged me to stay. She whispered, like she didn't want him to know."

"Know what?"

Patrice herded them a bit away from the body so the crime scene techs could set up.

"That she was afraid of him. I think. Just a guess. When he had his bags packed, she asked for his keys. He gave them to her."

"Did you sense hostility?"

"Ray. His name is Ray."

"Okay, good. How did Ray seem to you? Pleasant? Disturbed?

"A bit gruff, but nothing too overt. When he gave Marva the keys, he dug one into her palm, but his face was like 'no biggie.' Marva said she was changing the locks anyway. She didn't trust him."

Jane didn't look at the body again because the crime scene people had moved in and were covering it. Patrice asked her if she remembered what Marva had been wearing yesterday.

Jane couldn't remember. Her tongue felt thick, and she worried they'd think she was stupid. "I do know she was not wearing angel wings." She'd finally figured out what the shiny material on either side of Marva's bare shoulders had been. "I mean, those are angel wings. Right?"

Jesse had no comment, but Patrice said yes, angel wings.

The scene became crowded. Jesse was all business. He generally went into that mode when he worked a case. She wouldn't let it hurt her, even when Jesse asked a uniform to walk Jane back to her condo, but she would have liked a kiss, a smile, something. Life wasn't like that. It never had been. Jesse was who he was, and she liked him just fine. Most of the time.

What was it she'd wanted to ask Patrice? Last night, it was the last thing she'd thought of before drifting off, Jesse at her side. She couldn't remember. Her mind was not working properly.

She must have said that out loud. Patrice replied, "You're in shock, sweetie."

"Oh. I am?"

Kim walked onto the paved area just beyond the bayou grass. She called something to Jane. Then another neighbor and more yet until there was a crowd. Jane walked into the comfort of her people. Patrice followed.

"What's going on?" Kim said.

Other people were also talking, but Jane only heard Kim. Jane started to cry. She was happy Jesse hadn't seen her fall apart this way.

Kim grabbed Jane's hand and walked with Patrice on the other side, both of them propping Jane up, moving her along.

"What the hell is going on?" Kim said to Patrice.

"Marva's dead. On the bank."

Kim gasped. "By the condos?"

"Across the bayou," Patrice said. Since the bayou

27

really was winding, there were spots where buildings three and four had a bayou view. Jane and Kim were in building two, which backed up to Orange Blossom subdivision. White fencing contrasted with green trees, palm and pine, some in bloom with magnolia, some shedding their oldest leaves.

"It's happening all over again," Jane said. "Isn't it?"

"You think she was murdered?" Kim said.

Patrice was silent, but in Jane's mind there was no doubt.

"Maybe she took something, like MDMA. Didn't those people wear angel wings?" Jane asked. She didn't want to be involved with another murder. Maybe it wasn't murder. So, a drug OD? She tried to hold on to that thought, but it crumpled. Marva was not young and wild. The drugs she used were probably for constipation or cholesterol.

"We don't know anything yet. And probably won't for a while," Patrice said as they walked up the stairs to Jane's condo.

A few months ago, an outsider artist Jane admired had been murdered on Orange Blossom Avenue. That's how she'd met Jesse and Patrice. Jane knew murder when she saw if.

Jane unlocked her door and stood for a moment, looking at her mermaid mural in the long hallway. It always soothed her. Kim followed Patrice, who went into Jane's galley kitchen and filled the tea kettle.

Jane pushed away images of Marva's body lying there on the bayou. She wouldn't think about it until the kettle whistled. She walked down the hall and into the sunroom where Kim sat on one of the love seats. Patrice was still in the kitchen, fussing with a tray. She had been at Jane's place often enough during the last investigation. They were friends. As if to prove that point, Patrice came around from the kitchen and handed Jane and Kim tea sugared for the shock. The three of them sat and drank.

"Did it look like she was murdered to you?" Kim asked Jane.

"Yes. She was posed. If she'd collapsed from some natural cause, she wouldn't have been laid out like that. And she was wearing those angel wings. Frida Kahlo has a self-portrait with angel wings."

Jane went to her shelves and brought out all the Kahlo books she had. Ah, here it was. The diary. Frida, drawn with colored pencil? Crayon? Her hair was purple, and her wings were turquoise with black jagged slashes on the book cover. Winged brows slashed across her forehead. Loosely translated, Frida had written, "Are you coming? No. Broken wing." This alluded quite clearly to her homebound situation. And in another way, it fit with Marva, who was entirely broken. Dead.

"I don't know if the murderer was aware of this work by Frida. The entire diary is like a coded message. But the angel wings seem like a big coincidence," Jane said. Then she explained to Patrice and Kim about her visit to Marva's penthouse and the discovery that a Kahlo "original" was fake.

"Yeah, why would Marva wear angel wings?"

"Maybe the murderer put them on her," Jane said.

Kim's phone rang. "Good morning, Hazel."

Jane could only hear one side of the conversation, but she was sure she'd heard the whoop of an ambulance. They'd be taking the body away. She'd tuned out Kim and sipped at the sweet tea Patrice had set in front of her.

Kim hung up from Hazel, and Patrice made a stern

face. "We do not know she was murdered."

"I think we do," Kim said, undaunted by authority. Patrice didn't even wear a uniform anymore since she'd become detective.

"Are you okay?" Jane asked Patrice, finally remembering that Patrice's husband had moved out and her parents had moved in.

"Why wouldn't she be?" Kim wanted to know.

Patrice huffed out a breath. "I'm getting a divorce," she told Kim. "And yeah, I'm okay. Most of the time."

"Have some tea with us."

"Thanks, but I've got to get back to the scene. Stay here, okay? Jesse is going to want to ask you some follow-up questions."

"I'm not going anywhere," Jane said.

As Patrice let herself out, Kim said, "I need to go see Hazel."

"Okay," Jane said, but Kim didn't leave.

"That Marva...well, I hate to speak ill of the dead, but she wasn't a nice person," Kim said. "Hazel's been there. For dinner. More than once. They were pretty tight."

"Oh. How's Hazel taking the news? You told her?"

"I did. And I promised to go sit with her for a bit. You don't mind, do you?

"No, dear. I'll be fine. I may have to go to the station to sign a formal statement, since I discovered the body."

"Good thing you were with Jesse all night. Perfect alibi."

Jane hadn't thought of that.

Chapter Six

Hazel's nerves felt like they were outside her skin. Ethan had been gone when the murder happened. Stargazing, he'd said. She clicked her phone off, wondering where Ethan was now. She walked past the second bedroom, which was where he watched sports or other things. The bedroom window faced the pool. He was there, at his desk, making notes about the meteor shower, she presumed.

"Ethan."

He didn't respond, lost in his own world, the one in his head that she was not privy to. People didn't realize that sometimes you can be married and be lonely, too.

Hazel had left the screen door open, and Kim walked in with a shout. "I'm here."

Hazel left Ethan, who had not looked up from his notebook. She needed the hug Kim gave her.

"Where's Ethan?" Kim asked.

"Taking notes on the meteor shower last night. It was a big one."

"I wonder if he saw anything. Was he on a picnic table with his blanket?"

Hazel nodded.

"He didn't mention anything, but that's not unusual. When he writes his notes, he's only concerned with the sky."

Kim bit her lower lip. Hazel could read her mind. If

word got out that Ethan had been stargazing before dawn, he would be a suspect.

"I have to tell the police," Kim said.

"Oh, please don't," Hazel begged. "Ethan is a good person. He has his quirks, but he's always been a pacifist. He was a conscientious objector during the Vietnam war." Something he never talked about, not even to Hazel. He'd been beside himself for a week when their bird, a parrot, died. "He never would hurt a fly!"

"Did I hear an ambulance?" Ethan came out of his study.

"Marva's dead!" Hazel said. She studied Ethan as she told him.

His eyes widened, and he said, "No!"

"Yep, just about the time you were out looking at the sky. Come to think of it, pretty close to the same area," Kim said.

The implication went over Ethan's head. He was quite a literal person.

"Honey, Kim thinks, and I think she's right, that you should tell the police you were out and in the area at the time she died," Hazel said.

"Well, but why? I didn't hear anything. No screaming or gunshots."

"It looks like she was killed elsewhere and then positioned at the edge of the bayou."

"Unfathomable," Ethan said after a tense few minutes. "But if you think I should tell them I was out, I will. Except…Wait. How do they know when she was put there?"

"I don't know if they have that information yet, really. But it won't take them long. Ethan, it would look better if you got ahead of this thing and just admitted you were outside at what time? It was dark, am I right?"

"Yes, the best viewing time for meteors is just before dawn. Dawn was at 6:02 a.m. this morning. I like to get out there an hour or two early. It takes a while for the eyes to adjust to the darkness."

"So, was it an hour? Or two?"

"More like ninety minutes, last night."

"Well, they're going to want to speak to you."

"If you think I should, I will," Ethan said again.

"I think you should," Kim said.

Hazel didn't say anything. Her unfazed husband caused numbness to run up her arms. She sat on the sofa.

Ethan sat next to her. He patted her hand. "It's okay, honey. I didn't kill Marva."

"I know," Hazel said. She didn't know a hundred percent because nobody ever really knew anyone completely. But she was maybe ninety-nine percent sure.

"Okay, then, I'm going back to Jane's. The police are questioning her because she found the body. And identified it," Kim said.

"Do they think maybe *she* did it?" Ethan asked. "She hasn't lived here that long."

"Her boyfriend is a police detective, and they discovered the body together. He'd spent the night."

"Okay, well, should I go with you, or will they want to come over here?"

Kim pulled her phone out of her back pocket. "I'll call over there and see."

She talked to someone. Hazel didn't know if it was Jane or the boyfriend cop or someone else, but it was a short conversation, and after she stuck her phone back in her pocket, she said, "Sit tight. They'll be over soon."

****

Hazel said a reluctant goodbye to Kim as police detectives Riley and Singer, or as Kim called them, Patrice and Jesse, rang the bell. She waved them in through the screen door and nodded toward the kitchen table.

Ethan had wandered back to his office. Hazel wished he'd stayed with her. She didn't enjoy being around cops. Her father had been a high-end car sales manager who started into drugs, eventually became an addict, and lost his job. He'd often been questioned by the police at the family home, as had Hazel. Dad had gone to jail twice for drug busts. Her mother, trying to cope with two kids and a worthless husband, turned to alcohol. DUIs ensued. Hazel knew it was illogical to hold a grudge against the police for her rotten childhood, but she did anyway.

The three of them pulled out chairs and sat. Hazel tried not to appear a sullen teenager being asked about her father's drug use or her mother's drinking habits. Eventually, long after it mattered to Hazel, her folks had sobered up and became pillars of the rehab community, working at a halfway house in the city. By then, Hazel already had a job at the local college and her own tiny flat. Then she'd met Ethan, who represented stability. He was practical, predictable. Mellow. And sure, a little weird. Quirky was a nicer word for him.

"Is your husband here?" The female this time. She supposed they still took turns.

"Yes. In his office." She gestured toward the hallway.

"Where did you and your husband meet?" Jane's boyfriend cop asked.

"At work," Hazel said.

Ethan taught astronomy at the community college where Hazel toiled in the basement as an admissions clerk. She stuffed envelopes until computers came, and then, a few months after she started having lunch in the cafeteria with Ethan, she was encouraged to take an early retirement. She left the college, but not Ethan.

"This might go faster if I speak to your husband in his office, and Detective Riley will ask you a few questions here, Mrs. Pentress."

Hazel nodded. She fought her face, attempting cool neutral while wanting to cry. She slid from her chair and led Jane's boyfriend down the hall. She didn't like him one bit. She didn't much care for Jane, either. Marva and Kim had been her special friends first. Then Jane arrived and ruined everything.

"Honey, this is Detective—" She looked at him as Ethan spun away from the telescope. He loved the wheels on his swivel chair. Little things gave him a lot of pleasure.

"Detective Singer, Mr. Pentress."

"Please call me Ethan." He gestured to the chair tucked under his desk and smiled at her. Ethan had no problem with cops. He seemed a hundred percent at ease with the detective. Good.

Hazel walked back out to sit with the woman cop. Riley. She looked mixed Vietnamese. They were everywhere. Most Asians in St. Pete were Vietnamese. Every nail bar, every spa, every hair salon. They spoke awkward English, and conversation was difficult. But you couldn't get away from them. Some spoke better English than others. Riley's speech was impeccable. No accent whatsoever. And with her last name, she'd been born here. Marva had said Asians liked the weather in

Florida. She'd miss Marva. Her eyes welled.

"Are you originally from Florida?"

This could not be happening. Ethan was a good man. "Wisconsin."

"When did you move here?"

"Five, no, four years ago." When the babies left the nest.

Life had been perfect here, until now.

"When did you meet Marva?"

"We were both in the library and started chatted about our favorite authors. We joined the book group; it meets once a month." Marva had been more fun than anybody else, even Kim, because she was a catty gossip and Hazel took guilt-free pleasure in all she learned about the residents of Winding Bayou.

"And did you know her husband? Did you socialize as couples?"

"Some."

Hazel had been worried about Ethan, who had struggled to make friends or find hobbies. He tried a few of the many activities in Winding Bayou, didn't like any of them. He had his astronomy and took up kayaking on Coffee Pot Bay, where he made a keen study of the manatees, until he found a male friend he could tolerate: Ray, Marva's husband. The foursome went out to dinner and had each other over for meals. Ray was not interested in manatees or stars, but he liked to remark on women's bodies. Servers at restaurants, new widows, married women, even their daughters. Ethan seemed to enjoy the locker-room talk as much as Hazel did Marva's snide gossip. Harmless. They even got Marva and Ray to attend the weekly dances where they sat at a table for four, drank wine, and listened to cover bands play music from their youth.

Then Ray and Marva broke up. Ethan had been restless and without focus. Kim had said that Marva's breasts were bare. Dread she didn't want to name inched up Hazel's spine.

****

After the cops left, Ethan got out the scotch.

"Yes, please," Hazel said.

They settled into cushioned wicker chairs in their lovely sunroom. They'd played cards here at the round wicker table with Ray and Marva after dinner sometimes. And once, Scrabble. Hazel beat everyone so bad they never wanted to play with her again.

Hazel loved Ethan. She knew he was different, but that didn't bother her. He rarely opened a conversation but always replied to her questions. He'd been an excellent father. They didn't say anything as they sipped their scotch, a rare activity at this early hour of the day. Finally, Hazel asked her first question. She knew now how to pull information out of him question by question. She couldn't just say, "What happened in there?" because Ethan would say, "We talked."

"Did he look out the telescope window? Did he mention the pool?"

"He may have glanced out the window. I wasn't looking at him. But before he sat down, he took a peek through the scope. Didn't even ask. I had it pointed at the Orange Blossom subdivision fence line."

Hazel nodded, and they sipped.

"You told him about the comet shower last night and where you were?"

"Yep."

"What else?"

Ethan sipped his scotch before answering. "Not much."

"Come on, Ethan. Every question you can remember."

"Well, he wanted my exact times. And he did ask if I heard anything, but I didn't. So that was really it."

"Did he mention our friendship with Ray and Marva? Because I bet that Jane—he's her boyfriend, you know—told him we were tight."

Ethan drained his glass.

"I said we were friends and had dinners and whatnot. He asked what Ray and I talked about when you ladies discussed books and things. I told him about the boobs."

"What!" Hazel got up and poured them each another finger of scotch, sloshing a bit more in her glass.

"Well, Ray liked looking at women, especially boobs and butts. You know that. It's not a secret. Bound to come out. So, I said, as a friend to Ray, I developed an interest, too. Just boobs, not butts. For Ray's sake. Because he didn't care for astronomy or manatees." He finished off his scotch in two pulls. "We done?"

"Yes," Hazel said, draining her own rocks glass.

Chapter Seven

Jane was surprised to learn, as Jesse and Patrice were leaving her condo, that Patrice, now single, was going out swing dancing with Kim in Largo that night. Jane had watched a video online when Kim had asked her to come out swing dancing before she'd started dating Jesse. It was the only invitation from Kim that she had not accepted. She didn't have the coordination, which Kim was able to see from Jane's trouble with the fancier line dances, like The Matador.

Jane was a good dancer—she loved to dance—but she was crap at following syncopated footwork like that. And with a partner twirling her dizzy? There was just no way. Still, she was happy for Patrice. She'd told them what she could about Marva. She said word was Marva had unofficially put the penthouse on the market. She had no children but a sister and nephew in Everglades City. Jane then explained the fake Frida Kahlo fiasco.

Patrice stopped Jesse.

"L-look around Jane's living room at all the Frida art." She led Jesse back inside. "You've had that one of her with her monkey for a long time, but when did you get that one?" Patrice pointed first in the living room, then the dining room area next to the galley kitchen. "And that one?" She waved a hand toward a third, smaller Kahlo on the short wall dividing the living room from the sunroom.

"Well, I got the self-portrait with her monkey when I first moved here, downtown at that art print shop just off Central. It's a print, you understand. Not valuable. And then the one in the niche, that was a memento of when we all went to the exhibit. I found the antique frame for the big self-portrait downtown in one of those funky shops. Isn't it gorgeous?" Jane loved the hint of gilt around the circular depressions that bordered the black-walnut Mediterranean frame. She'd had fun choosing the double mat, maybe a half inch of gold showing below the bright blue. The art print shop downtown had a website, and she'd ordered the glass and matting from them.

"I did my dining room for Thanksgiving, but the walls were bare. I didn't want to do too much. You saw how Marva had her art wall?"

Jesse and Patrice nodded. They'd told Jane crime scene was working the penthouse, but they'd taken a quick look at the art wall. Jesse had taken a photo of it on his phone, which he handed to Jane.

The fake Frida was missing from the wall. "Oh!" Jane said. "It's gone. The fake Frida."

Jesse gave her a minute to sip her cold tea, then he flashed another photo of what he called "a big-ass bowl" in the middle of Marva's living room.

Jane was on the case. "It's art glass. Not a Chihuly, but a decent piece in his style. Just a few air bubbles on the rim. Still, it was plenty heavy enough to bash somebody in the head." She wondered, but didn't ask, if it could have been the murder weapon. There could be blood on the bottom of the bowl, but wouldn't the murderer clean it up? Her job, as art consultant to the St. Pete police, was to answer questions, not ask them, yet her mind played out a scene: Marva hears a noise; someone is stealing her Frida painting; she picks up the bowl to hit the intruder...but somehow, and this was where the image dissolved, Marva was hurt instead. Killed.

Patrice and Jesse remained silent, waiting for Jane to continue her Frida dissertation. Jane wondered in a single freaked-out moment if she was a suspect. She couldn't be. She'd been with Jesse all night. "So I got that print." She pointed to the far wall in the dining room. "It was a special order. Frida's first self-portrait. She'd painted it for a lover, a man who left her, and she wanted him back. She wooed him with her work."

"Well, no monkey. No mustache. But the eyebrows are there," Partrice remarked.

"And really long fingers," Jesse added.

"She kept monkeys as pets. They are a motif in her work second only to the eyebrows. But before that, early career, she worked in the style of Modigliani."

The detectives looked at each other and shrugged.

"Not important to the case."

"Let us decide that," Jesse said.

"She was still imitating the Surrealists, hadn't fully developed her unique talent yet. She was nineteen years old when she painted that."

Jesse shoved his phone into his pocket.

"I told you it wasn't important to the case," Jane said.

He smiled, but she could tell his mind was miles away.

Patrice had moved over to the third Kahlo in the room, which was simply a poster of the event Jane had attended with Queenie and the art group.

41

"So yeah, that's from when we went to the exhibit a few days ago. Marva was there. It was the first time I met her. She told me about her recent acquisition of an original Kahlo, which is big news. Kahlo originals rarely come up for sale, and they are way beyond my price range."

"She looks pretty in this one," Patrice said, "with the flowers in her hair and the ribbon."

"That's a photo," Jane said.

Jane had all her Frida books, that's how she thought of Kahlo to herself, as Frida, gathered on the coffee table in the sunroom. She opened the big one of the self-portraits on the bar that separated her galley kitchen from the sunroom, Jesse and Patrice on either side of her. She stopped here and there to point out the way Frida titled her portraits with a kind of banner. She pointed out the stylized signature.

"Why would someone steal a fake Frida?" she asked herself aloud, not expecting any hypotheses from her friends. "Do you think the forger was trying to destroy evidence of his crime? Like, stole it back and killed Marva?"

"That's one of dozens of possibilities" Jesse said. "We still don't know the murderer stole the painting."

Jane didn't know much about art forgery, except it was rampant. "It could be a perfectly legal reproduction that Marva lied about."

"I could go to Taos and take Jane with me," Patrice offered.

Jesse's eyes flashed with interest. "That's FBI jurisdiction," he said with regret.

And then he hustled Patrice out the door.

Chapter Eight

The next day, Kim talked Jane into walking down to the clubhouse for coffee. Jane had a hard time believing they hadn't canceled after the murder yesterday.

"Did Jesse call you after he finished work last night?" Kim asked as they walked down Winding Bayou Boulevard toward the clubhouse.

Neither of them looked toward the nature path Jane and Jesse had walked just yesterday morning. Jane shuddered, remembering Marva's body a little off the path, closer to the bayou than the condos, where police tape marked the perimeter of the murder scene. Long stretches of the bayou were fronted by swamp mosses and cypress trees. Frogs on lily pads croaked.

"No," Jane said. Jesse had not called. It was petty of her to be disappointed about that; she had to manage her expectations better. He could dump her if she got too clingy. But…shouldn't she be herself? Not change for him? Being clingy was a change. She'd been more independent in her marriage. Way more. Well, she'd learned to be. It felt better not to cling. Not to care.

"Maybe they're still searching," Kim said. "I see activity over there."

Jane didn't look. Jesse wouldn't be there. Patrice wouldn't be there. Detectives didn't do the dirty work, Patrice had told Jane when she'd still worn a uniform herself. She'd waited for Jesse to call, or to at least text, until almost dawn. Then she'd fallen into fitful sleep until Kim's call woke her.

"Maybe," Jane said, as they approached the heavy Mediterranean-style doors to the clubhouse. The fountain in the center of the gated courtyard spurted merrily, not a drop of water daring to land on the ornate polished tiles.

They donated their dollar, and Kim raised her hand to wave at the widows, who, Jane noted, had saved two seats for them. Hazel was at the table as well, dark circles under her bloodshot eyes. Jane knew how worried she must be after a visit from the police yesterday. Hazel's husband, Ethan, wasn't there, but he never came to coffee. Too busy checking through his telescope toward the pool for young visitors in skimpy bathing suits, Jane thought.

The clubhouse was packed, every seat, every table, full. The buzz of a hundred low-toned conversations filled the air.

"Am I imagining it or has the volume escalated since we walked in?" Jane asked Kim as they walked toward the coffee urn.

"Well, you found the body."

"Yeah." Jane shivered.

Nobody approached them as they walked to their seats. She took the seat between Queenie and Kim, who'd dropped off her coffee and was heading for the donuts. Jane said a general hello, noting the only man at the table. Randy. Natalie's husband.

"Ever since you moved into town, there's a murder every week." Randy smiled.

Jane wanted to stick her tongue out at him or give him the finger. Instead, she sat on her hands. "Ha-ha," she said.

"Your boyfriend's so good-looking," Queenie said.

Jane focused her smile on the artist, the first she'd cracked since before she and Jesse had found the body. And it was genuine, although she couldn't take credit for Jesse's gorgeousness. People were born with beauty. The rest worked with what they had.

Kim came back with an apple fritter and plopped in her seat. Jane was comforted by Kim next to her. Kim made her feel safe. Not that she normally felt unsafe. She risked removing her hands from under her legs to slurp coffee in one of the new paper cups. The Bayou had started a recycling program. No more Styrofoam. Yay.

"Yeah, he is," Jane answered Queenie, her wide smile growing tired.

"Hope he catches that killer today," Natalie said.

Jane wished she had one of those pills her doctor had prescribed, but they were home in the medicine cabinet. She wished she was lunching with her mom, listening to stories about the flute player Dad was rehearsing some new material with. "Wild Thing" by the Troggs, "Goin' Up the Country" by some band that had played at Woodstock, Jethro Tull tunes Jane couldn't remember the names of, if she'd ever known them. She looked around the table. These were her friends. Most of them. Natalie was nice, but she didn't know her well. Right now, Nat looked ready to throttle Randy, who was flirting with Kim.

The widows were being polite, but Jane saw the questions in their eyes. "Listen, ladies, I don't know any more than you do. I haven't talked to Jesse since it happened."

"He was up at your place for an hour, I heard," Hazel

said.

"How long was he at your house?" Jane shot back.

Hazel paled; Kim kicked Jane's foot.

"Sorry, Hazel. I just meant the police have likely interviewed all of us, am I right?"

The widows nodded their heads.

"I'm not going to see him until they catch whoever did this. And if I do speak to him, I know not to ask about an ongoing investigation."

"But…about the art that was stolen when Marva was killed…won't he talk to you about that?" Queenie said.

"That's part of why he was at my condo yesterday. I doubt I can help the police any more."

"But it's a connection. You saw Marva's art hours before she was killed. A priceless painting was stolen, and my best friend is dead! You may have been the last one to see her alive," Hazel insisted. She gave Jane a hard look, squinty eyes and all.

Jane stayed mum even though the killer had been the last to see Marva breathing. She kept quiet about the "priceless painting" turning out to be a fake, too. "Her assistant Abigail was there when I left," Jane finally said. "You should know, being Marva's best friend and all."

The widows murmured in agreement with Jane. Hazel's face turned blotchy, and she burst into tears. That took everyone's attention off Jane as heads from other tables craned necks toward Hazel. The widows tried to comfort her.

Jane wondered if everyone assumed Ethan was Suspect Number One. If they all thought she had the "real" scoop. The Bayou grapevine had obviously been informed, likely with more rumor than fact. Jane leaned into Kim's ear. "I have got to get out of here."

Kim patted Jane's arm. "Okay, kiddo."

Jane stood, said a quick and general "bye" to the table, and scooted out the door, around the corner of the clubhouse, and into the sunshine. Hazel and Ethan's condo faced the pool on the other side of the clubhouse, and Jane shivered as she thought of Ethan peeping out his office window with his telescope. Was he looking at her now? She didn't relax until she got past their building. Even then, she race-walked home, her mind a blurry whirl.

She slowed as she reached the steps to her unit on the second floor. God, that Hazel was a piece of work. Jane didn't meet anyone on the steps. Nobody on the walkway either. Beth's storm door was open, Fox News blaring due to Beth's husband's refusal to wear hearing aids. George and Barb's unit was quiet, door shut. Barb had been suffering from morning sickness, poor thing.

Jane reached her door and, while unlocking, looked over to 204. It would likely remain vacant until after Christmas when the snowbirds flocked down. There were two more condos on her floor, but she didn't check to see if the lady who walked her two cats on leashes was out and about. She'd learned the woman's name was Rusty and she'd lived in Orlando her entire life until Disney took over the town. Rusty was nice but quiet. She kept to herself.

Jane mostly did the same, well, except for yoga with Beth and dinner at the Boathouse with George and Barb. She line-danced with Kim and the other widows on Tuesdays. Saw her folks at least once a week. She still loved hearing her dad play guitar. He never worked in November or December, by choice. But come January, he'd find a gig. He always did.

She looked out her sunroom window. The coffee and donut crowd streamed out of the clubhouse. She saw Kim, her arm around Hazel, walking her home. Good. She'd been a bit sharp with Hazel. She should try to be nicer. Ethan was strange, but that didn't mean he was a murderer. Jane's deceased husband had been strange, too. Well, more like they'd been estranged. They'd stayed married for the kids, but Stan had worked all the hours he could, and then worked a few more. Jane stayed busy with her own lecturing life, which had involved lots of travel and research into art history and the artists' lives. It hadn't been strictly academic, looking into the lives. But that's what fascinated her. Life informs the art, she always thought. That was especially true in Frida's case. As for Jesse, overwork was a trait he shared with her former husband, and that made her nervous. Maybe he'd call later.

****

Despite a heated conversation between two women Jane did not know, she approached the mailboxes. As she slid the key into her box, the two women stopped shouting long enough to shoot her twin nasty looks.

Ah. She did know one of them. Abigail, Marva's assistant.

"Just, you know, getting my mail," Jane said, instead of rolling her eyes at their public spat. "How are you, Abigail?"

Abigail didn't reply to Jane's question. Instead, she said, "You found Marva, right?"

Jane grabbed her mail and shut the box. She scanned Abigail's face, but the young woman's expression was inscrutable. "Yes. I'm sorry for your loss," Jane said.

She wished she'd never seen the fake Frida painting

on Marva's wall. Maybe Marva would still be alive. She caught herself linking the fake painting and Marva's death again. Why did she keep doing that? When she moved to St. Pete, did she suddenly develop psychic powers? She didn't feel like a psychic. Now that she no longer used her talent for talking about art, other areas of her brain were beginning to light up. Not psychic. Intuitive.

"You!" the other woman said, startling Jane. It wasn't like she'd killed Marva. She'd only found the body. And she hadn't even been looking.

Mystery female and Abigail were somewhere in their early thirties. Unusual for this community. They were both wearing shorts and thin sleeveless tops. In the first week of December. It was a nice day; Jane wore flip-flops because they were easy. Her long jeans and cardigan over a T-shirt were more weather-appropriate, but she shouldn't judge. Let the young people do their thing. Meanwhile, Abigail was saying something to Jane about Marva's mail.

Mystery female yelled, "It's Ray's mail, too. And he's alive. Give me that key, you bitch."

Ah, Jane thought, this must be Biffy, Ray's new woman.

Kim walked up. She and Jane met at the mailboxes most days.

"What's up, ladies?" Kim's tone telegraphed that they were the opposite of ladies. She'd probably heard the shouting from her condo.

"Are you Biffy?" Jane asked.

Biffy nodded. Her long bleached-blonde hair, the color and consistency of straw, didn't move. Florida's humidity, even in December, required super-strong hairspray, and Biffy took full advantage, whereas Abigail's hair was soft and shiny and moved with the breeze.

"So, Kim," Jane said, "this is Abigail, Marva's assistant, and Biffy, Ray's girlfriend."

"Fiancée," Biffy snapped.

"Okay."

Biffy and the equally bellicose Ray deserved each other.

"They both want Marva's mail," Jane told Kim.

"But the police will have already taken possession of the mail, am I right, Jane?" Kim asked.

Both young women's eyes narrowed. Abigail jammed the key in Marva's slot while Biffy was distracted. She turned it, but it didn't open.

"Yes, I think the police have the only access to Marva's mail now," Jane said, wondering if she'd gotten that right. She did not ask Jesse or Patrice about their work, and they didn't offer. They did, however, ask for help with any art-related aspects to their investigations.

"If Ray's living with you, Biffy, he should have his mail forwarded." Kim was ever helpful. And practical.

Biffy wilted. "He is, but sometimes mail addressed to both of them comes to my house, so I figure some stuff comes here to Ray. Like his paychecks. I get my paycheck deposited straight into my bank account, but Ray's old-fashioned. Doesn't trust banking that way. I tried to show him how to take a picture of a check and deposit like that, and you'd think I'd asked him to participate in a human sacrifice." Biffy stopped and slapped her hand over her mouth. She gave Abigail some side eye as she removed her hand from her lips. "That didn't come out right. I'm a wreck. You try being a single mom with a kid. I can't afford to support Ray, too."

Jane felt bad for Biffy. Bitches with bad hair had problems, too. "How old is your son? Or daughter?"

"Ozman is seventeen." Biffy sniffed. "He's at a delicate age. I'm determined he's going to turn out right, starting with college."

Jane wondered if Ozman and Ray got along. And if Ozman was a real name or if Biffy's kid was a fan of Black Sabbath. But she didn't say that, instead she said, "Call the police station and explain your situation." Jane hadn't liked Ray the only time she'd met him. He would be the kind of guy to keep his paycheck, lie about it, and live off a single mom.

"Did you know the penthouse is the murder scene?" Abigail asked Jane. "I can't get in to water the plants or look through Marva's email."

"The police always take the computers and phones, dummy." Biffy sniffed again.

"They said they're going to call when I can come up. To give a statement," Abigail said.

"I'm going too," Biffy said. "I can ask them about the mail."

Jane patted Abigail on the shoulder. Without any provocation, an image of the fake Chihuly bowl displayed on Marva's antique piecrust table popped into her mind. So what was the image of the bowl trying to tell her? Was it really a possible murder weapon? That made sense. She'd had the same thought before. Abigail and Biffy both seemed too thin to heft it. But their arms were toned. Especially Biffy. She probably did fifty planks a day.

Kim retrieved her mail and stood next to Jane. "We

51

done here?"

"Yep."

They walked away, waving at the young women.

"I have no idea what Biffy sees in Ray."

"Except a paycheck that keeps getting lost in the mail," Kim said. "Want to come over and have a glass of wine?"

"Yes," Jane replied. She worried Patrice and Jesse might want her input on the painting, but why? Well. If Ray found out the painting was a fake, if Marva had gotten ripped off royally, would he get mad enough to clobber his wife with a gigantic bowl?

Glasses of wine in hand, Jane and Kim discussed these burning questions.

"I think you ought to tell Jesse everything about the fake Frida," Kim said.

"I fully briefed him and Patrice. Well, as much as I know. I need to figure out if that painting was a legitimate reproduction and if Marva said it was an original to puff up her reputation as the art collector of Winding Bayou."

Chapter Nine

After Kim left, Jane called Jesse, who was up in Marva's penthouse.

"I'm looking at the art wall," Jesse said, "and just like in the photo, there's no painting like the one you showed us in the diary on here. It's nowhere on the premises. Wait, Patrice, does that spot right there look like maybe a painting could have been hanging there?"

The homicide detectives conferred.

"Are you free to come up for a minute?" Jesse said. "We're not sure if the picture is missing or not. Kind of hard to tell. At least in museums, they space the art a little bit."

"Yeah, it's a hodge-podge." Jane preferred well-spaced art walls, like museums. "I'll be right up."

Jane hung up the phone and finished the last sip of her glass of wine.

"When you get done with the cops, I'll pour you a refill," Kim said.

Jane hugged her friend. She was getting a headache. Maybe wild ideas about murder did that to a person. "Okay, well, I'll text you when I'm finished up in the penthouse, but I'll probably go home for a nap."

"Suit yourself, but you know I refuse to drink alone before dark."

"What about the pool? Happy hour?"

Kim walked Jane to the door. "You're right. Happy

hour doesn't count. You wanna come? I bet I know what the main topic of conversation will be."

"Keep your ears open. I can't do happy hour. Discovering Marva's body wiped me out, and I didn't sleep well last night." Jane opened the door and stepped outside. "Plus, if I do more than one happy hour per week, my jeans don't zip."

Kim giggled and waved her off.

****

Jane saw the empty spot on the art wall the minute she walked in. Same as in the photo. "It was right here." She pointed without touching. "I noticed it was missing in your photo, Jesse, but I thought maybe these guys"— Jane pointed to the evidence techs swarming around the piecrust table where the fake Chihuly bowl had sat in dishonest splendor—"had been examining it."

They gingerly went over every inch of the bowl with gloved hands. The bottom of the bowl, which had been yellow and green yesterday, was stained with a splotch of something darker. The table had been chalk-painted white; now it was smeared with red.

Jane's stomach flipped like a pancake. Her knees weakened, and she swayed but managed to stay upright as her eyes swept the hectic colors and clashing frames of Marva's art wall. "Nope, it's not here. Nobody placed it on a different spot on the wall." She grabbed the lounge chair in the little television area just behind the art wall. It was a rocker and almost knocked her over.

"You okay?" Jesse said.

Jane nodded.

"I'm almost done here. May I come down and take a statement from you? Like how you knew the painting was a forgery? And why that bowl"—he pointed to the art glass—"almost made you faint?"

Jane nodded. "I've got a little headache, and I'm going to meditate for a bit. Just use your key."

"Sure thing."

A uniformed officer came up to Jesse and said something Jane didn't hear. Other voices, Patrice, and maybe Abigail, came from the kitchen. She didn't want to know. She needed to go. She waved at Jesse and left the penthouse. She took the special elevator to her ordinary condo, popped two ibuprofens, and stretched out on her sofa, closing her eyes and trying not to think. Just focusing on her breath. In and out. It didn't work for more than a few seconds. That was normal. She noticed she was thinking and let the thought go, over and over again. It was amazing how long you could think without even knowing it.

****

Jane didn't fall asleep as she sometimes did when meditating, so she heard Jesse call out "It's me!" when he came in.

"And me," Patrice said.

They came through the hall, and Jesse helped himself to a bottle of the soda that Jane had started stocking when she found it was his favorite beverage.

"Patrice, you want a St. Pete Special?" he said, holding the fridge door open.

Jane, who sat up from savasana and tidied her hair with her fingers, smiled at Patrice. People complimented Jane on two things: her complexion and her smile. She smiled a lot; it was automatic.

Jesse sat on the sofa next to Jane and gave her a quick kiss.

"I know the answer already, but does this mean I

won't be seeing much of you two until the homicide is solved?"

"Sorry, Shug," Jesse said.

"You know how it goes." Patrice winced.

What Jane knew was that the first twenty-four hours were crucial. She should make sandwiches. She tried to remember if Jesse had finished off his favorite cookies last night.

Patrice set her phone to record. Jesse opened his phone notepad.

Jane went over the day at the penthouse, Jesse asking questions.

Then Patrice said, "How long have you known Hazel?"

"Oh, I guess I met her when I met Kim and everybody else at coffee. Hazel comes to everything. Dance, art class, um, not yoga."

"Know her husband?"

Jane had a brief inner debate with herself before she told them Ethan and Ray had a creepy way of discussing women's bodies. Even if the women were there. "I remember the first time I met Ethan, he said I had 'a nice pair.' He's not very social; that's about the only comment he's ever made to me."

Jane and Jesse exchanged a look.

"Hmmm." Patrice mused. "The way the body was posed, with the breasts exposed, it's an interesting coincidence."

Jesse told Jane that in most rapes, the lower half of the body is often exposed. "So, this is already different."

Jane picked up the Kahlo diary. "Under the title text block, in the actual portrait, Frida's breasts are exposed."

"And the angel wings look quite similar," Jesse said,

looking down at the book. "Except for the bowl, that's all we've got. So, Jane, what led you to think the bowl was the murder weapon?"

"I had a flash image. You know what I mean?"

"No," said Jesse.

"Yes," said Patrice.

"Well, Jesse, it's like a quick thing, like a memory but not. Because I never saw it. I just flashed on the image of the bowl being raised."

"But not who raised it?"

"No. Sorry."

"Women's intuition, dude," Patrice said.

Jesse nodded.

"So some person stole a fake painting, murdered the owner, and posed her as Frida," Patrice said.

"That doesn't sound like anyone here in Winding Bayou, if you eliminate boob-happy Ethan," Jane replied. "He's weird, but not murderously weird. I have a feeling the bowl was the murder weapon. Ray seems more like he could heft that thing than Ethan. Also, Ray had a key, but Ethan didn't. Marva had not changed the locks quick enough. And Ray could drag Marva down to the bayou."

"Do you see Ray as someone capable of not just murder, but posing a scene from a fake painting right down to the angel wings?" Jesse asked.

Jane did not. Ray seemed too pugnacious for dramatic touches.

"It could be a false lead. Someone plants clues that might point to someone else," Patrice said, her eyes pinning Jane under their questioning gaze.

"I have no idea who that could be. What about Abigail?" Damn it. There she was being intuitive again.

The words had popped out before she could stop them.

Jesse and Patrice clearly saw the puzzling connection between Frida and the murder. Jane and Jesse's relationship was still new. She didn't want him to think she was a crackpot by talking about the mental images that had popped up. Cops got intuitive hits all the time, Patrice had once told Jane. They just called them "gut feelings," and that way their masculinity was protected.

Jesse and Patrice got up as one unit and shut off their phones. "Call us if you find anything else out."

Patrice walked down the hall. Jesse hung back to give Jane a hug and quick kiss on the cheek. He was already out the door before she remembered she had been going to make them sandwiches.

Chapter Ten

Jane, loaded down with bags from the grocery store, slowed as she reached the second floor. She stood still for a minute, taking in boxes, lots of moving boxes, a few doors down. Jane lived next to George and Barb's place, which was quiet, window shades down, door shut. If the ex-FBI agent weren't existing on soda crackers and ginger ale, Jane would ask her about how local police would go about tracking a murderer who maybe stole a forged painting that Marva had said she bought in Taos, New Mexico.

What was with the moving boxes? Jane walked past Barb and George's toward her own unit. The boxes were stacked on the walkway in front of Unit 203, right next to her place. Jane unlocked her own door and stepped inside. She stood there waiting to see what would happen next. Two guys in work uniforms appeared and took boxes toward the elevator; two others moved out a battered leather sofa. Then a lumpy mattress. Out with the old, in with the new. That happened a lot in Winding Bayou.

Jane shut her door and locked it. The FBI had had an undercover guy staying there a few months ago to protect George when he had been targeted by criminals. She had to call Barb. She brought up the number on her phone and clicked it. She walked into her living room as Barb's phone rang, one, two, three rings.

Barb said, "Hi, Jane." She sounded fine.

"Hi, honey, sorry to bother you, but do you know, did someone buy 203? Will they be living there? A moving company is cleaning the place out. Is the FBI going to use it again?"

"I don't think so. Let me make a few calls. I'll get right back to you."

Jane paced the living room. She couldn't sit. Now she was waiting for two people to call. He'd been so good about calling and texting and keeping in touch. It was a daily thing. Or had been. Jesse would probably not keep in touch like he had been now that he had a murder to solve. So why was she destroying her confidence in their relationship with her crazy demands for closeness? She had to stop it. Predictably, Barb was much faster reconnecting than Jesse. It took her less than an hour to phone Jane back.

"Stockbroker from New York bought it last week. He owned a piece of one of those firms on Wall Street, but he sold his partnership, so he's loaded. He's married—maybe trouble in paradise, because she's not on the Florida title, still living in their swanky Manhattan pad. He's staying with friends somewhere in North Carolina until the place is up to his standards, which explains all the racket down there. Two kids, both in Ivy colleges. The wife does charity work, and not the stuffing-envelope kind. Basically, she shops, gets her hair and nails and who knows what else done, sees Broadway plays, and pays thousands of dollars to attend her favored charity's fundraising dinners."

"Thank you. That explains why he's not living in Palm Beach."

Barb laughed. "Divorce is expensive."

"Thanks so much for getting back to me so quickly."

"Yeah. I still have a friend or two left in the Bureau."

"How are you feeling?"

"Sick as a dog. Thanks for calling George about this new crime in our backyard."

"Déjà vu again."

"No kidding. Keep us posted."

****

Jane lay on her sofa, listening to the commotion next door. Lots of work being done, but so far, no stockbroker. And no Jesse. She learned from the television that Marva's killer was still at large.

Meanwhile, next door, there'd been painters in, new bathroom fixtures installed, right down to the toilets and pedestal sinks, new lighting throughout, new kitchen cabinets. Today it was new floors. Jane knew this because some of the contractors worked for other people in Winding Bayou, who told Kim. Between Jane and Kim, they checked out print and pictures on boxes delivered. The stockbroker hadn't appeared, but the floors would only take a few more days. Would he have someone furnish it for him? Buy sheets and plates, a coffee pot and cutlery? Or would he do that himself? Would he be here by Christmas?

Jane had been looking forward to Christmas with Jesse. They hadn't said "I love you" yet, but Jane knew she loved him. She thought he might love her, too. It felt like love when they were alone together. Jesse's tenderness was something she hadn't even known she was missing. Now she craved his kisses. But the romance had happened fast. They met in October, and she'd invited him to Thanksgiving with her friends and family. Before Marva's murder, they had planned to be together at least part of Christmas day, depending on his job. They'd talked about exchanging gifts. Jesse was all for it. He was too good to be true. "Just the two of us," he'd said.

Jesse had a few nice watches, and she'd bought him another one and wrapped the box, put a bow on top. It was waiting for him under her pretty white tree with white lights and gold ornaments. After he caught the killer, he'd be back. He had to come back. She was in deep. Addicted. Had she ever felt that way about Stan? She didn't think so. Almost on autopilot, she picked up her phone and texted —*Are we still on for Christmas?*—

His reply was short. —*Let me get back to you. Xo*—

The Xo helped.

Someone knocked on her door. After briefly checking the camera, she flung it open. The suit and tie gave him away. Mr. Former Stockbroker had arrived.

****

Crabby Grant sent frequent warning emails about so many things. No wearing a bathing suit without cover-up to or from the pool. Men were not to go bare-chested. Not hanging beach towels on the walkway railing. Not keeping lawn chairs or even a mat outside your front door. People did all of it anyway.

Once stockbroker Dennis had introduced himself, he asked Jane to step outside where he'd set up two beach chairs, a small table with wine in actual glasses, and a charcuterie tray. This wasn't abnormal, but it was against Grant's rules, so Jane had never done it herself. Still, it would be surly to say no to his invitation. It had to be past noon by now. And she was curious.

Jane sat with Dennis, and they toasted to new neighbors.

"I heard you're from New York." He didn't have an accent that would give him away like many of the snowbirds.

"Yes. I wasn't born there, but I worked on Wall Street, so…"

"My son's a broker on the Street."

"Wow, small world."

They chatted about where her son worked and sipped wine slowly. Neither touched the crackers. Jane nibbled a lush strawberry; she had totally forgotten she was tired and planning a nap.

"This is absolute bliss," Dennis said, turning his face into the sun. "Do you know how cold and snowy it is right now in Manhattan?"

"I do. I lived my whole life in Detroit until eight months ago."

A short silence fell between them, and then Jane told Dennis about all the workers that had been in and out for the last several days. "They would have made your little picnic area impossible. It's nice of you."

"Kind of like back in the day, when people used to sit on their front porches instead of hiding on their back patios."

Just then, George peeked out of his unit. "This the new guy?"

"Dennis," said the stockbroker.

George didn't need further invitation. He brought along his own beer and beach chair and set up across from Jane's door. If Cat Lady came out to walk her darlings, she wouldn't be able to pass.

"Dennis, this is my good friend and neighbor, George."

"You're not over fifty-five," Dennis said.

"Hello to you too," George said. "I'm not. A few of us youngsters are allowed to be interviewed, and my wife and I passed with flying colors. Management thinks it's good to mix things up."

"Where is Barb?" Jane asked. She was so glad George didn't mention Dennis's suit. He'd taken off the jacket and tie and rolled up his cuffs. But of the three, he was the only one in actual shoes. He probably didn't own a pair of shorts. He was in great shape for his age. Almost as fit as Jesse. So he must have workout shorts. Jane curtailed her wandering thoughts and tuned back into the conversation.

"She's lying down." George turned to Dennis. "My wife is pregnant."

"It's their first baby," Jane said.

"Enough about me," George said. "What's a fancy New York stockbroker doing in this dump?"

"George! It's not a dump!" Jane protested. Then she took a healthy sip of the smooth Chardonnay Dennis had provided.

"That's a funny story," Dennis said. "I got a tip on the penthouse prelisting from a Realtor pal. I made an offer, packed up my stuff, and was on the plane before I knew it was no longer available. Don't know who bought it or how they beat me to it."

George and Jane shared a wide-eyed glance.

"What?" Dennis said.

"I heard it had been up for presale," Jane said, "then the owner died." She didn't say the word murder. "Her divorce wasn't final, and I think maybe the husband is moving back in?" Well, that sounds like a motive for murder, Jane thought, but did not say. Did Jesse know about this? He must.

"Anyway, I already had a friend working on furnishings and things, so I bought this condo and had her spiff it up. I like it," Dennis said, shooting a look at George that said *dare to differ and you die.*

From there, the discussion went as most first meets do. Jane and Dennis both had kids, and Jane had a granddaughter. Jane was a widow. George was a newlywed. Dennis and his wife were separated. His boys were in college. They'd been threatening to bring all their friends down for spring break.

"The beaches here are really nice," Jane said. "Over a hundred miles of uninterrupted white sand."

"I've been here before," Dennis said. "My dad lives here. He is in his eighties, and he's been in and out of the hospital so much I figured I'd just move down."

"Where's your mother?" George asked.

"They're divorced. She lives in New Jersey, where I was raised."

"My parents are still healthy," Jane said. "They live down here. My daughter's in Seattle with her husband and my granddaughter, and my son's wife is pregnant, too. In New York."

"His hours must make her crazy."

"Not really. His father was the same, and she knew it when they got together. She's a reader. A professional reader for the publishing industry. She's been picking and choosing what she reads now. She plans to stay home with the baby for a year."

"Jane reads like a fiend," George threw in.

"What kind of books do you like?" Dennis asked, pouring more wine in Jane's empty glass.

"I was reading murder mysteries for a long time. Now I'm stuck on historical novels."

"Ahh," Dennis said. "I like the thrillers. Stephen King is my hero."

"And I," George said, "read the newspaper. Online." He took the last sip of his beer and closed his chair. "Was good to meet you, Dennis. Jane, see you soon."

"Does Barb need anything?"

"Nope. We have ten boxes of crackers and two cases of ginger ale."

"Okay." Jane wished George had stayed a bit longer. She wanted to see Dennis's house but not on her own. How could she get a look inside?

"So, you had someone decorate. Did they buy all the things you need to cook and clean?"

Dennis laughed. "I'm not much of a cook. I hired a cleaning service. They do my dad's place, so I knew they were good. They do laundry and windows, and they leave dinner when they're done. Likely the only home-cooked meal I'll have all week."

"There's loads of seafood places. Great salads. People seem to eat healthier here than in Detroit."

"Do you go out to dinner often, then?"

"Not every night. I make a huge salad and eat it all week. Some days I'll be creative and throw in some chicken or shrimp. Then I usually go out with my parents or friends on the weekends. I get my steak fix, as I don't cook it." Jane realized Dennis had not answered her question about the decorator. Where was Kim when she needed her? Kim could weasel info out of anyone, even a fancy New York millionaire.

She must have been quiet too long, because Dennis answered like he'd read her mind.

"About the decorating. I didn't mean to avoid your question," Dennis said. "She did basics, but I plan to finish things myself. I like contemporary art, and St. Pete is a great town for that with all the little galleries. I'm taking my time with it. Otherwise, I've been choosing off the internet, so a bed, pillows, and sheets were here when I arrived. I've ordered a nice television and recliner being delivered tomorrow. Football season, you know."

Jane hated football, but she didn't hold it against him. Dennis could eat, drink coffee, even work on a laptop with one recliner. As long as he had a side table. She heard her phone ring; she hadn't brought it with her. "I should get that, but it's been nice meeting you."

"Nice meeting you, too, Jane." He handed her a card from his wallet. His old business card, but it had his cell number on it.

She wondered if Dennis was dating. What was the story there? Had he or his wife cheated? Or did the marriage just fizzle? Too personal to ask about any of that now.

"Thanks for this. Management has a phone book out every year. You don't have to list your number, but I do. I'll add your number to my phone and send you a quick text so you'll have mine."

"Okay, that would be great."

"Once you're settled in, my friend Kim and I can show you the best beach spots. If you're a beach guy."

"Well, I did live on an island for a few decades. Not known for its beaches, though."

Jane laughed.

Her phone had stopped ringing a few minutes ago. It started up again.

"I better get that. Thanks for the wine." The mellow vanilla notes of the wine lingered in her mouth. "It was *so* good."

"You're welcome. I'm looking forward to meeting Kim and seeing the beaches."

"It's restaurant row down on Gulf Boulevard."

"I'd love to treat you ladies to dinner."

"It's a date!" Jane said, feeling hopeful for Kim. Should she say she had a boyfriend? Weird thing to call your lover at her age. She skipped it for now. She got up from the chair, waved and opened her storm door, but the phone inside stopped ringing again. All she could think about was Jesse. What if he'd been calling her? She always kept it with her "just in case," and the one time she didn't…she picked up her phone from the table by the sofa. Kim. Both times.

Her heart hurt. She had to stop thinking about Jesse until the crime was solved. It was unfortunate that she was so sensitive to men (one man, really, her deceased husband) who forgot about her when they went to work, men who always worked. But Dennis didn't work. He liked art, was an amateur-photographer, phone-pictures-only type of guy. He wanted to watch sunsets and shoot pictures to catch the flash of green light that some lucky people had seen just as the sun set. Jane had seen pictures of the green light, but she'd never seen it while watching the sunset.

Dennis was nice, and he was retired. He was good-looking and liked the idea of being nothing but an art-loving beach bum. But she was saving Dennis for Kim, if they hit it off. What did separated mean, anyway? Was Dennis dating? He hadn't flirted with her, she didn't think. Had he?

Chapter Eleven

The minute she got back inside her condo from her visit with Dennis, Jane called Kim. "Sorry I didn't pick up before. I was having wine with my hot new neighbor."

"You've got news; I've got news. Yours is better, you go first."

Jane told Kim all about Dennis, all being the little she knew. "Now what's your news?"

"Hazel told me Marva changed her will, and Ray is out. Her sister and nephew get everything," Kim said.

"Wow." Could that even be legal? Marva and Ray were still married, after all. Jane wondered how Hazel knew about the will being changed. Why it was just coming up now, and did Jesse know? She felt shy giving him Bayou gossip. She was much more confident sharing art information.

"So how did Hazel know?"

"The police visited her again. Not Jesse. Regular guys in blue. They are having another go at Ethan as Suspect #1 because Ray and Biffy were together all night the night of the murder. They want to pin the murder on Ethan."

"That's too bad. I don't believe he did it, and I know you and Hazel are close."

"You can help her, can't you?"

"I can try. For you. So what about motivation? Ray seems like he has *more* motivation than before. And

69

Biffy would lie for him if it meant she could keep her rich fiancé. Also, Ray has his own money, am I right?"

"I don't know. See, that's why you need to come with me next time I talk to Hazel."

"I'm not sure she will want to talk to me."

"She will. She admires you."

"She has a funny way of showing it."

"That's just Hazel. She's insecure."

And that was Kim, always helping insecure, lonely, isolated people. Jane had been one of them, after all.

"It seems unfair that you're bookended by handsome men and I have widows on either side of me."

"Dennis is great. Charming and kind and easy to talk to. He's retired, too."

"Do I hear a hint of longing for the new guy? Is Jesse going to be flung out of your life because he's doing his job?" Kim said.

It wasn't a bad idea if she could be practical about things. But she wasn't. For better or worse, she was in love with Jesse. She'd give him another day. Or year. "I'm not breaking up with Jesse. I like Dennis for *you*. He's almost perfect."

"Almost?"

He's got lots of money but also lots of expenses, which is why he's living here with us middle-class folk."

"Sounds sketchy." Kim didn't trust men much, but they all loved her.

"Just meet him. I told him we'd show him the beaches, and he invited us out to dinner for some fresh-caught grouper at a beach restaurant on the Gulf while we watch the sunset."

"Girl, you need to get out more," Kim said.

"That's what I'm doing. I'm planning to get out with

you and Dennis. He's really very nice."

"Then why bring me along?"

"I'm in love with Jesse." Jane had moments when wished it wasn't true. They evaporated whenever she pictured his face with those Tampa Bay blue eyes.

"Everybody seems to know that but Jesse."

Jane sighed in agreement.

"Okay. I'll meet Dennis if you help Hazel."

"Deal."

They hung up after making a time to meet at Hazel's.

****

Jane and Kim walked across the wide boulevard to Hazel's. Christmas lights decorated the royal palms planted down the boulevard in perfect symmetry. A soft wind blew, tingling bells on Santa's sleigh propped on the wide lawn in front of their building. December felt strange without snow, but she'd get used to it.

She said hi to Ethan as Kim and Hazel went into the kitchen. Jane, alone with Ethan, sat and put her hands in her lap, listening to the whispers and giggles of Hazel and Kim. Ethan ignored her, reading a print magazine called *Astrophysical Journal of Letters*. He seemed thoroughly engrossed and had not looked at Jane's boobs once, which was good. But also bad because she needed to ask him some questions that might clear his name.

"Interesting reading?" she said.

"Yes." He continued reading, not looking up from the printed page.

"What's it about?"

"Oumuamua."

"What's that?" This was almost as bad as talking to Stan. He held up the photo from his article, and she had to move across the room to view it. She sat on the sofa beside him, hoping Hazel would not think she was flirting. Since she'd become a widow, she'd learned women were quite protective of their husbands around her. As if she wanted another one of those. Well, she hadn't until Jesse. What? Was she thinking long-term already? Banish the idea. Too soon.

Finally, after finishing his paragraph, Ethan spoke, answering her question about the Oumuamua. "It's a mysterious UFO in our solar system that some believe is an interstellar object, discovered in 2017, in the skies above Maui, with the help of a powerful telescope. At first it was exciting, as it seemed there was no way this mysterious object had gone undetected in our solar system for so long. It's reddish and cigar-shaped, close to a mile across and five or ten times longer than wide."

Good. He was talking, his face animated. He seemed to be enjoying himself.

She had to keep him talking. "So, a cigar-shaped comet."

"Yes, but it moved through space in a funny way for a comet." Ethan held out his hands and wobbled them.

Maybe if she acted interested in Ethan's comet, she could get him to open up about other things. Like his relationship with Marva. What would his motive be? She'd divorced his only friend for being a serial cheater who moved across town to shack up with his latest lover? Ethan was weird, but not murderous weird.

Ethan handed Jane the magazine, turned to the page with a photo. She'd never seen a comet shaped that way, but it didn't look anything like a spaceship of the sort dreamed up by science fiction writers. But she had the magazine and Ethan's attention.

"I understand the police questioned you again."

"Yes."

"Are you worried you'll be arrested?"

"No." Ethan kept glancing at his magazine.

Jane tucked it between the sofa and her thigh so he couldn't grab it and go back to reading.

"Why not?"

"I didn't do it. It's true I was out and very close to where Marva's body was found, but everyone knows I was looking at falling meteors."

Jane didn't say what she was thinking. *Not everyone: not your wife, not Kim, not the police.*

"Ray believes me."

Ray. According to Kim, Ray had steered the police toward Ethan.

"And Ray had more to gain from Marva's death than I did. Much more."

That was true. Unless the dubious new will was legal. Jane thought about the angel wings. "I found her," she said.

"Yes. I knew that."

"She was stripped to the waist except for a pair of angel wings." She checked but no reaction from Ethan.

Whoever had killed Marva had to have known about the painting and that it was a fake. Whoever killed Marva had read Frida Kahlo's diary. They'd left those wings to say exactly that. Jane didn't think Ethan killed Marva. He wasn't the type to read diaries of dead artists. Who was? Find that out, and maybe she'd find the killer. Still, what was the motive? A taunt? To whom? Nobody but Jane linked Marva's death with the angel wing painting.

"So I'd heard."

Jane startled out of her thoughts. "Where could

those wings have come from?"

"I believe she purchased them online. For a Halloween party at the clubhouse."

So the wings belonged to Marva. Which meant whoever killed her had knowledge of her home, even down to the fact that she owned a pair of angel wings. That pointed to Ray, except he seemed even less inclined to read diaries of dead artists. Marva hadn't read it. She hadn't even heard of it. The forger would know about the connection between the fake painting and the wings. It was easy information to look up online if you knew what to look for. Maybe Marva's assistant, sweet Abigail? Or Biffy? They both had access to Marva's closets. Yet everyone had seemed clueless about the wings. Not just where they came from, but why the killer, or even Marva herself, had put them on like a costume. Someone was a good actor. Not Ethan. He had been silently telegraphing his need for the science journal ever since she'd tucked it away. But he did know about the wings.

"This Halloween?"

"No."

Jane sighed. Interrogation was heavy work.

Kim and Marva came in from the kitchen with a plate of finger sandwiches, another of cookies, and a pitcher of iced tea and glasses. Also, napkins and little plates with palm trees decorating the rims. They set everything on the empty coffee table.

"Hazel, do you remember when Marva wore those angel wings to the Halloween party?" Ethan asked his wife. His voice warmed when he spoke to her.

"I do!" Kim said. "I can't believe I didn't remember. It was four or five years ago."

Jane mulled this over. Why would Marva keep a

74

costume that long? On the other hand, the penthouse was plenty big enough.

"Jane, I want to show you something," Hazel said. She was looking out the screen door at a group of teen girls giggling, heading to the pool. Jane stood when Hazel did.

Ethan ignored them as he reached across the sofa cushion and carefully extracted his scientific journal. He ignored the girls. Ignored Kim, too, for that matter, as he searched for his place in the article.

Hazel led Jane into the guest room. A telescope aimed at the window facing the pool, a desk, a chair. Not a thing on the surface of the desk except a closed laptop. "Did you see those girls?" Hazel asked.

"Yes." Jane nodded.

"Those young ones are like red meat to Ray."

"I've heard," Jane said.

"Look into the telescope. Careful not to move it," Hazel said.

Jane did so. The lens focused on a bird sitting on a nest in a tree. "Cute."

"Ethan has been waiting for those chicks to hatch almost from the time the parents built the nest," Hazel said.

Jane stayed quiet. Let Hazel get to her own point.

"My husband bonded with Ray by taking an active interest in what Ray liked. Boobs. Not threesomes!"

Jane had heard about the threesomes. "Okay…," she said.

"Ray liked a young girl in bed with him and Marva. He put up with Ethan and me because Marva liked us and that was her compromise. She conceded to his desire to be a pervert, and he acted friendly couples with us."

"How young?"

"Oh, twenty or so. He wouldn't break the law with jailbait."

Men could be such pigs. Jane just wanted to go home. She'd hurry this story along. "Abigail?"

"Yeah, then Biffy. Now Marva's dead, he wants Abigail and Biffy to step up."

"How do you know this?"

"People talk," Hazel said. "Even Ethan. At least he talks to me."

"Do the police know this?"

"It didn't come up, but I don't mind if you tell your boyfriend. Ray's so busy trying to get two young ones in his bed, he's totally ignoring Ethan."

"How are the chicks doing?" Kim said, coming into the room.

"Still inside their shells," Jane said.

"Did you find something to clear Ethan?" Kim asked.

"Ethan didn't kill Marva. I don't have proof, just a feeling. And I did find out all about the Oumuamua."

She didn't say her plan was to find a better suspect than Ethan. Like Ray. He looked guilty as hell. That was not her job, but maybe she should tell Jesse about the sexual shenanigans and let him look into Ray.

Chapter Twelve

Jane and Kim walked across Winding Bayou Boulevard toward home. Like so many days, it was perfect blue-sky weather. Warm but not burning hot. "What's a good day to take Dennis around town and up the Gulf a little way?" Jane asked Kim.

"Don't fix me up, Jane."

"No, of course not. It's just…He's so charming. And handsome."

"Sounds like you want to date him yourself."

Jane sighed. If Jesse didn't at least text a heart soon, and if Kim really wasn't interested, maybe she would. She immediately scolded herself for the thought. She was projecting too much of Stan and their long, horrible marriage onto Jesse. That's what her mom, a former therapist, would say. Also she had news for Jesse, so what the heck, she'd call him.

As they reached their building, a bright orange sports car came screeching down the boulevard, smoking tire rubber so hard it made her eyes water. The speed limit in the community was fifteen; this guy was doing more like fifty.

"That Ray is a menace. I guess Marva didn't get the locks changed after all. And the penthouse must not be a crime scene anymore," Kim said as Ray pulled into his garage.

Jane tucked that information away. Somehow all

these crazy pieces must add up. The sooner Jesse and Patrice closed this case, the sooner they'd get their lives back.

"Let's get the mail," Jane said.

Ray's garage was located next to the mailboxes, but he used his private elevator entrance and went straight up to the penthouse. Jane was glad. She didn't want to see that piece of slime. It was so clear to her that he was guilty. Of killing his wife and other crimes. The husband always did it.

Kim said she had to get her key, and they split off.

Jane opened her mail slot and pulled out mostly junk just as the garage door to Ray's place opened. She closed her box and stood there, still and quiet. She could hear someone with Ray. Biffy, probably. They were arguing about something, she could tell from the tone. The words were not discernable; everything but one word was too muted. That word: *Abigail*. No surprise Ray and Biffy fighting about Abigail. No surprise Biffy was jealous of Abigail. She had good reason.

Kim came back into the covered mailbox alcove with her key on a pink chain with a Hello Kitty button on it. Ray's garage door shuddered closed.

Jane gave Kim a quick hug. "I better call Jesse and Patrice and tell them what Ethan told me."

"I thought it was about UFOs? Or comets?"

"It was, mostly, but the threesomes, well, that's new info to the cops."

"Not to me," Kim said. "Ray is slime, and the husband always does it. He has a motive. I bet Marva wouldn't do the sex things anymore."

"I think so too, but the police have to prove it. This should get them off Ethan's case, however."

"That would be good. Meanwhile, I'll keep my eyes and ears open," Kim said.

****

She hesitated to call Jesse. He liked her to stay out of his cases except when he needed her. He worried she'd be a target. That proved he cared, didn't it? Love as an older person wasn't any easier than it was for young people. Maybe Ray had only wanted to knock Marva out with the bowl. When he realized he'd killed her, he…put angel wings on her? Carried her down to the bayou hoping nobody was out for a predawn stroll?

Jane left a voice mail on Patrice's phone when she didn't pick up. Did Queenie, a friend, an artist, a lovely woman, know about Frida's diary? It seemed quite likely. Queenie had no obvious motive or means to kill Marva. But she'd probably read Frida's diary and knew about both pairs of angel wings. Queenie had been the one to invite them all to the Frida exhibit. And she painted. Could she have forged that Frida for Marva? For a price? Maybe under an assumed name through a go-between? Because Marva was truly shocked and angry when Jane told her the painting was a fake. She reluctantly decided to talk to Queenie. At least that was art-related. She shivered and went to find a sweater. It was not cold, so why was she chilled? Was Marva pushing her to talk to Queenie from the other side?

****

Jane steeled herself. Neither Patrice nor Jesse had called. She sipped tea and decided to get her courage up and text him. She'd tell him how she felt. Well, she wasn't going to say she loved him. That should be said face to face. After he said it first, if possible. How about she liked him a lot, but she needed more from him if he wanted her to hang in there? If he couldn't call her before he went to bed, could he at least text her? She typed it out, hit send, and grabbed her lawn chair. She set it outside, next to her door. Then she poured a glass of wine into her plastic goblet, tucked her phone into her pocket, and went out to catch some sun.

She settled into her lawn chair. Ray was the obvious suspect. So why hadn't Jesse arrested him? His alibi was thinner than a fashion model. She sipped her wine and brooded. Had Jesse come to the same conclusions about the killer she had? Improbable. When would Jesse call? When would he text? There were only fourteen days until Christmas.

Dennis came up the stairs hauling a Christmas tree. That was sweet. Jesse didn't bother with a tree, and Jane hadn't thought it was her place to push him into it. She'd told Jesse he could share hers. Before the murder, he'd agreed to Christmas dinner at her place and even suggested they exchange gifts. That had to mean something.

"Let me help," Jane said to Dennis, setting her wine glass under her lawn chair.

"Thanks," Dennis said, dropping his key into her hand. "Can you get the door for me?"

Jane opened the door and followed Dennis into his remodeled abode. She and Kim had been so wanting to see it. Fabulous, as they'd imagined. The wood floors gleamed. The ceramic tiles in the hall, kitchen, and sunroom added subtle touches without being fussy. The marble countertops screamed money. Or male with money. The furniture, what little of it he had, all looked custom-made. A coral-and-green-striped sectional fit perfectly into his main room. An art glass floor lamp knocked her socks off. The stainless-steel appliances were mellowed a notch by cupboards in a rich cherry wood.

He dragged the tree into the formerly empty sunroom and fit it into a stand. The sunroom, with its big window, was a showplace for the tree. Jane breathed its sharp tang of pine.

"Thanks, Jane," he said.

She hardly heard him. She grabbed the black marble bar that flowed into the kitchen countertops so she wouldn't fall. Her legs didn't want to hold her upright anymore.

Marva's Frida painting hung on the wall between the kitchen and the sunroom. It was still in the same frame.

Chapter Thirteen

"I quite like it," Dennis said, "for a reproduction."

Jane quelled her panic. Dennis was not a murderer. He hadn't even been in town the day Marva was killed.

As far as Jane knew.

"Where'd you pick it up?" She turned to face him. She wanted to see his eyes in particular. She could always tell a liar by their eyes.

"Don't take this the wrong way," Dennis said. "I'm not a flea-market kind of guy. I like new. But the gilt frame caught my eye, and I've never seen a repro of any of the paintings from the diary, so I bought it at a church rummage sale."

His eyes were twinkling, and not a shred of guilt flicked over his face.

"Really? The one down on Park?"

"Yeah. I got lost. I went down Park Avenue instead of Park Street. I pulled over to set my GPS, and there was the church and a banquet table heaped with crap. I noticed the way the paint on the frame glinted in the sun. It's not my usual style, but somehow it called to me." He flushed. "That sounds stupid."

Jane noted his flush. Blond-haired men were attractive, although they did tend to redden when angry or embarrassed.

"Not stupid at all." Jane pretended not to notice his blush. "How much did you pay?"

"Twenty bucks."

"When did you purchase it?"

"Yesterday. There's so much practical stuff to buy. But I dislike blank walls. So far, I've been to Marshall's, Costco, Target, and Rooms-To-Go. Good for house stuff but not so much for art. I haven't warmed up to any particular artists in the galleries yet. I need to visit a few times. The appliances came with the kitchen remodel, but this painting, it's nice. At a church rummage sale of all places. I'm still not done! But for now, Frida warms the place up."

Dennis didn't know Jane was a former art lecturer. It had not come up. "I'm quite a fan of Frida myself. Good to know you are too." Jane smiled, but her mind was racing. Dennis had read Frida's diary? He was a nice guy; she was sure he didn't steal the painting from Marva's, even though he could have been in town before he moved next door. How would he get into the penthouse anyway? And what would be his motive? She didn't think he was the murderer. Was he?

"You seem to know her work quite well. This painting has never been exhibited."

Dennis shrugged. "I read a review of her diary, the one they found after she died. I was interested enough to buy the book. My soon-to-be-ex-wife and I love art. And in New York, we had museums and galleries and street art. We loved it all. Sadly, art alone cannot hold a marriage together."

Okay, that all sounded good and true.

"I have bad news." She didn't know how to say it any other way. "I'm calling the police. That painting was stolen from the penthouse, and its owner is dead. Murdered."

She'd already selected and clicked Patrice's number.

"Wait," he said, when he realized she was calling the police.

"I can't. Oh, hi, Patrice. No, that first bit was me talking to Dennis, my new neighbor. He found the stolen Frida painting at the church rummage sale. The one on Park Avenue."

"I'll be right over," Patrice said.

"We'll be here."

Jane clicked her phone off.

"Jane, what the hell is going on? What murder?"

"The murder and the stolen painting and you moving in happened kind of at the same time, and everything was in disarray. I'm sure mentioning a possible homicide in the building slipped the board's mind. Her funeral, Marva's, the dead woman, isn't even until tomorrow."

"My God."

"I hope you're on Her good side, because this is serious." Then Jane explained the events of the past few days.

Twenty tense minutes later, Patrice called out through the screen door.

"Come in," Dennis yelled.

"You'll be okay. Patrice is nice. And the dead woman's husband is looking like the main suspect." Jane took no pleasure in knowing Dennis was now probably a suspect, too. And it was her fault.

Patrice came into the living room, Jesse following. Oh sure, he had time to follow Patrice around but no time to phone her, his girlfriend. Lover. Whatever. Maybe ex.

"Jane!" Jesse said. "Patrice told me you called." He

handed her the plastic wine glass from under her patio chair, gaudy with tropical pink flowers.

"Thanks." Jane kept her voice neutral as she introduced everyone. Her wine was warm.

Dennis swiped it from her hand as she lifted it to drink and went into the kitchen. "Can I get anyone anything to drink?" He came back around the corner and handed Jane a chilled crystal glass of Chardonnay. The kind that slid down your throat and tasted slightly like butterscotch.

Everyone stared at the painting, even Dennis. "So, drinks?" he said.

"No." Jesse's curt voice sliced Jane's heart.

"I'll have a sweet tea, thanks," Patrice said.

By the time Dennis returned to the sunroom and distributed drinks, Jesse had his phone notebook out and Patrice was recording the painting. They stood at the bar since the sunroom was not furnished. Patrice asked Dennis if she could record their upcoming interview. He said fine. Jane was very glad to have a chilled glass of wine in hand. She took a large gulp.

"Jane, is this the same painting you saw at Marva's?" Jesse asked.

She let him wait while she swallowed her wine and examined the painting again. "Yes."

"Is it possible someone is making copies?" Jesse again.

"No, well, it's possible, but highly improbable. This is the same frame, and who would paint one fairly obscure picture over and over?" Jane raised her eyebrows in Patrice's direction.

"Okay, good, Jane. Thanks. You're free to leave," Jesse said.

"No, Jane, don't go," Dennis said. "This won't take long?" he asked Jesse and Patrice.

"No," Patrice said at the same time Jesse said, "Maybe."

"Jane, do you mind staying? I don't have an attorney down here yet," Dennis said. "And I was going to ask you to help decorate the tree. Also, I have wine. Your favorite."

"I'll stay." Jane wondered how Dennis knew her favorite wine. But he was right. This one was quickly outpacing her usual twenty-dollar bottle.

"That is one lovely Chardonnay, am I right?"

"You are!"

"Now, Jane," Jesse said.

Jane held her hand up like a stop sign. "I'll just sit in the living room quietly while you ask your questions. You might have one or two more for me. You never know."

"Thank you, Jane," Dennis said.

Patrice subtly checked Dennis out and then winked at Jane.

"Dennis, you might want to record the conversation, too," Jane said, stretching out on the clever chaise section of the sofa in the living room. The glass in the floor lamp looked different colors of blue from different angles. It reminded her of beach glass.

"Good idea," Dennis said. Then he excused himself to get a coffee.

"Jane? More wine?"

Jane's glass was more than half full. "If I'm going to help you decorate that tree, I better skip another wine." She listened to the conversation, next to the real pine tree. Her first Florida Christmas. They had to nail Ray before then, but the discussion was routine, and she learned nothing new about the murder.

"Bye, Jane," Patrice said when they were finished. In a low tone, she asked if Jane was free for breakfast.

By the time Jane agreed and they'd set a time and place, Jesse was already walking out the door, having shaken hands with Dennis, not even glancing her way. She stood up.

"Jesse," she said, following him down the hall. "Didn't you get my text?"

"I got it," he said. "I was going to text you tonight."

No apology, but Jane knew those were hard for Jesse when it involved work.

"Are you still going to?"

"Do you still want me to?" Jesse said.

"Yes. You said, 'was going to,' past tense."

"Maybe we need a phone call."

"That would be better."

"Just don't take too long drinking your favorite wine and decorating the new guy's Christmas tree."

"I promise. I'm not sure he even has ornaments."

Chapter Fourteen

Jane lay on the sofa reading about how Stevie Nicks had gotten pregnant by one of the Eagles and, instead of having the baby, terminated the pregnancy. Despite Jane's own disappointing marriage, she'd never regretted marrying Stan. He'd been the father of her beloved children, and for that, she'd always carry something akin to love in her heart for him. She did not judge Stevie, who chose career over children. Jane's children, and now her granddaughter, were the best things in her life.

She was so deep into the book and the thoughts that swirled with it, she didn't hear the front door open. When Jesse yelled out, "Honey I'm home," the book flew from her hands toward the ceiling and landed splayed on the floor. Her heart beat like a thousand drums in those few seconds. Jesse never dropped in unannounced late at night. And he never called her honey.

Her nightie was a little clingy. So what? He'd seen her in less. She picked up her book just as he got into the room. She smoothed the pages and used the book jacket fly leaf to mark her page. "I...hi. Honey?"

He scooped her up, hugged her, kissed her, and put her back on the floor. "Just mixing it up, Shug." He grinned. "Was going home and you were on the way."

She knew he wasn't. She lived east of the police department, and he lived smack on the Gulf coast. But she was not that far east of downtown. Had Dennis's screen door been open? Was Jesse warning him off?

He took her hand and led her to the sofa. Put his arm around her. "Sorry if I scared you or if you are not in the mood for company," he said.

"You are welcome any time. That's what the key is for." Would she ever see his place, let alone be given a key? She put her head on his shoulder, and after a few seconds, he lifted her chin and gave her one of his lazy lovely sizzley kisses. She melted into him.

"I love you, Jane," he said during a breathing break.

"I love you, too." It sounded strange to hear him call her Jane, but the word love rang just right.

"Okay if I spend the night?" He yawned.

"More than. I was just about to turn in."

He glanced at her book. "You and Dennis get his tree all decorated?"

"No," she said. "As I suspected, he had no ornaments. And on the way to buy some, he had to stop at the PD to sign his statement. Also he mentioned consulting his designer."

"Good Lord! For ornaments?"

"I know. But he's nice."

"Sure, but you don't love him. You love me."

"Damn right I do."

"I'm going to take a quick shower and have a shave." He touched her cheek. "I gave you a little razor burn." He kissed her cheek.

" 'Sokay. Meet you in bed." She picked up her book, and they walked toward her bedroom. He didn't have pajamas here, but she knew from experience he slept in the nude. And he had fresh work clothes in her closet for tomorrow.

****

The next morning, Jane and Patrice met at a breakfast place halfway between their two houses.

"How you doing, hon?" Jane asked.

"Okay with the divorce and family stuff. I wanted to vent about work to somebody, and you're the only somebody I know I can trust with this."

Jane reached over the Formica tabletop and took hold of Patrice's hand. "What is it?"

"So. A co-worker, Jesse's former partner in fact, has been harassing me. Nobody seems to notice, and he does it in the presence of others. Including Jesse. Promise you won't tell him?"

Jane nodded. "Of course." She figured it wouldn't be sexual harassment, not with witnesses. "Is it about gender or race?"

"Oh, both. He called me a China doll once. I'm not from China! I was born here, and my dad is white. My mom is half-Korean. They were both born here!"

Jane had not even known Patrice was biracial until Patrice had told her a few weeks ago. Her lightly tanned skin came from the Florida sun. Her pretty heart-shaped face had beautiful blue eyes. Maybe Jane was a bad friend not to immediately recognize that Patrice had less than one hundred percent Caucasian features, but did it matter? Only if another officer picked on her for it. So not right. "And Jesse didn't say anything when he called you China doll?"

"It was a briefing in a room full of cops sitting around a conference table. I'm not sure how many people even heard. If Jesse did, he never mentioned it. And it's more than that. He puts his hand on my shoulder and lets his fingers dangle in the air right in front of…right in front of…"

"Your breasts."

"Yes. I don't think it's a mistake. I've been keeping a log and watching him. He does put his hand on other cop's shoulders, all male, but he gives the shoulder a full grip. None of this dangling bullshit." Patrice's eyes filled, and tears traced their way down her face. She didn't make a sound, just brushed the tears away and moved her water glass as the server set their breakfasts down.

"I think it's good you're keeping a log. Shouldn't you go to internal affairs?"

"Cops are so old-school. It's not like TV. There's racism and sexism and every other ism, and they get away with it all the time."

Jane swallowed a bite of bacon and sipped coffee. "And you feel like you can't tell Jesse because?"

"Oh, he and his former partner are great friends."

Jesse would stick up for his new partner if he saw any of the actions Patrice had mentioned, and Jane said so.

"I know," Patrice said. "Thanks. But while I'm quite sure Jesse has seen, I'm not sure he's 'seen,' if you know what I mean."

Jane did know. "What are you going to do?"

"Keep a notebook and keep quiet. For now. Maybe he'll stop. I've thought about quitting, but, shit, I'm a single mother now. I just got my dream promotion, and I was the paycheck in the family, not my ex. He's actually demanding child support from me!"

Patrice was in a bad place. Jane didn't know what to say except "That sucks. Every bit of it."

"Yep. Anyway, it felt good to tell someone. And

maybe, I don't know, if we solve this case and Jesse gets back to normal—oh yeah, I know how the job consumes him—maybe I'll tell him and ask his advice."

"I hate for you to be harassed like this. I hate for it to be ongoing and Jesse being blind to it." Jane thought for a second. "Maybe if you have yet another brilliant solve under your belt, it will help when you take the dirty truth to your chief."

"I've been steering clear of my boss. Every cop is on this murder, so it's natural I would be out chasing leads."

"Good. God, I want to punch that guy in the face. What's his name?"

"Promise not to tell Jesse?"

"Absolutely."

"Tesper," Patrice said. "I got his job. I think Jesse requested it on Tesper's last leave of absence. He takes a lot of those."

The server brought the coffee pot to their table, poured them another after they both nodded, and took away their empty plates.

"Now tell me about the kids. And your folks."

So they caught up on the lighter side of life, if pending divorce was lighter, while they sipped their coffee.

Finally, it was Patrice's turn to ask Jane how things were going with Jesse.

"He told me he loved me last night," Jane said.

Patrice's face cleared. "We got a big lead last night on the case. I wasn't going to mention it, but your insights on the art angle really help. I think you deserve to know Ray and Biffy got married. And Marva never made a new will; it was a figment of Hazel's imagination. Trying to protect her husband, I'm thinking. Oh, and you know Ray and Biffy are living in the penthouse?"

"Wow. I had a feeling. Still, that's a lot. Is Abigail still there?"

"No. Ray wanted to keep her until she could get rid of all Marva's things, but Biffy refused," Patrice said.

"I heard them arguing the other day," Jane said. "Even before I told you and Jesse about Ray's little quirk in bed and what he wanted his new wife to do with her, I suspected Biffy was jealous of Abigail."

"Why?" Patrice asked.

"With good reason," Jane said. "Word around the Bayou is she and Ray had a thing. It didn't last, according to gossip, and it was before Biffy, but that was not good enough for the new Mrs. Battington. Abigail had to go."

Patrice's eyes widened before she put on her cop face. "Who told you this?"

"I have no idea. I could have overheard it. People here talk loud and don't seem to care who hears them. Or they've forgotten to put their hearing aids in. So it wasn't anybody talking to me, just people talking at coffee or cocktail hour around a big table. It's not a secret."

Patrice shook her head and glanced at her watch. "Thanks for the local hot topic. Do you remember if you heard this before or after Marva was killed?"

"I think both. Yeah, pretty sure it was both."

"I've got to go." Patrice reached for her wallet.

"I'm paying, remember?" Jane said.

"Well, okay. Thanks for breakfast and the pep talk and the juicy gossip."

93

Chapter Fifteen

At 11 a.m., Jane pulled into Winding Bayou and spontaneously parked by the clubhouse. She might as well check out Queenie today, while she was thinking of her. It was an art angle, even though Jesse was supposed to ask for her help before she jumped in. But he was busy. She'd just have a casual talk with Queenie. If Jane remembered right, this was the correct date and time for her art class. She stopped by the office on her way to the crafting room and blinked. Abigail was sitting in the office manager's chair.

"What happened to Bill?" Jane asked. Bill had been at Winding Bayou forever. He kept the place running. When she'd bought her condo, he'd done all the paperwork with her. Step by step, he walked her through what she needed to do to become an owner. It had been the first time she'd bought a house on her own.

"Hi. I'm fine. How are you?" Abigail said.

"Ugh, sorry, hi, Abigail. I'm just surprised. I've never seen anyone in that chair except Bill."

Abigail laughed. "It's fine. I was kidding. I'm temping while Bill's on vacation."

"I didn't think he took those!" Jane laughed, but she noted Abigail's "just kidding."

Most of the time when people said "just kidding," they were not. Not really. Abigail wanted to fit in as if it were perfectly normal to be here. Maybe it was about respect; she didn't want the first thing people said to her to be where's the other guy? The one I'm comfortable with? The one who is always here? Whatever, she tucked Abigail's passive-aggressive words into the file cabinet in her head.

"I'm wondering if I'm too late for Queenie's art class?"

"Are you signed in?" Abigail's eyes ran down a paper on a clipboard.

There was no sign-in for any class Jane had ever taken. You showed up or you didn't.

"Nope. You're not signed in."

"Queenie invites me to come every week at pool cocktail hour."

"Be that as it may, you need to sign in." She passed the clipboard to Jane, who dutifully recorded her name and handed the clipboard back to Abigail, whose hand was outstretched, waiting for it. Jane fought the strong urge to roll her eyes.

She walked down the hall past the fitness center and the billiard room. Queenie was sandwiched in between the library and the yoga room.

"Jane! Welcome! You finally came." Queenie held up a finger, indicating that she was helping a student and she'd be right with her. Queenie was going to be disappointed. Jane did not paint. She drew. With graphite pencils. For her, drawing was a way to let go. She knew about art because she'd studied it, taught it, and eventually fallen into a sweet lecture gig.

She admired painters; she didn't want to be one. Her thrill was studying other people's art. Like with Frida, you could see her pain in every brushstroke. Something about the way she held her head, the curve of her neck, her straight back in the self-portraits, reminded you of her story. Which wasn't pretty. She'd had polio as a child, and one leg was shorter than the other. Then when she was eighteen, she'd been on a bus in Mexico City on the way home from school with her boyfriend when it collided with a street trolley. A handrail pierced Frida's body, entering at her spine and exiting through her pelvis. She had many surgeries, years of recovery, much of it lying in bed. During these times, she painted. She used her damage and pain to create art. It was there to see, even without blood, thorns, or other painful adornments she sometimes painted onto her image.

Queenie came over where Jane had been standing by the door. There were half a dozen women in class today, everyone busy with their canvases, boards, brushes, and tubes of paints. The room smelled like linseed oil. Jane recalled Frida had used the old way of making yellow with egg yolk and linseed oil.

Jane touched Queenie's arm. "I'm not staying. I just wanted to see how you're doing. I know the police questioned everyone."

Queenie sighed and stepped outside the door and to the left so that her students couldn't see her.

"They're all absorbed in the work," Jane said.

"I wish you'd join us. You don't have even a bit of curiosity about how it feels to put brush to canvas?"

"It is a little weird, I guess, but my focus has always been on the art, and, sometimes, like with Frida, the way artist's private lives and their work intersect. I remember once my dad asked me why I dated so many musicians. This was before I married. He said maybe I wanted to be one. But that wasn't it. I like music and am interested in the people who make it, including my dad, but I really just wanted to dance. For me, paintings are the same. There's a dance between the work and the viewer."

Queenie scrunched her eyes. Then she nodded. "I get that," she said.

"My new neighbor found Marva's Frida painting at a church rummage sale."

Queenie blinked at the quick change of topic. "Oh wow."

"I know. I almost fell down when I saw it hanging on his wall."

"The new guy."

"Yep."

Queenie leaned her back against the wall hugging herself, her expression a mix of guilt and pride.

"Did you paint it?" Jane asked.

"Yes," Queenie said. "I didn't realize the person who commissioned it would be selling it as an original, but I put my mark on it just in case."

"Let me guess," Jane said. "The year 1955."

"Yup," Queenie said.

"It's a lovely reproduction."

"Thank you. I do several a year, not just Kahlo. Someone from an art shop, the kind you see in tourist towns, sends me an image, usually from a famous dead artist, and I paint it. It's a job." She sighed. "I'd rather be painting from my own soul, you know? And I do sometimes. But I need the big commissions to make ends meet."

"But you're at the Farmer's Market, and you've been downtown, in galleries, in group shows." Jane needed to introduce Queenie to Dennis. Stat.

"Yes, and I make somewhere in the mid-three figures on the sale of each of my originals most years."

She grinned. No biggie.

"I had no idea." Plenty of shops sold reproductions. She just hadn't known Queenie worked for some of them. "Were you able to help the police, I don't know, maybe locate the store where the reproduction had been sold?"

"They didn't ask about the painting, but it's not like I'm hiding what I do. Quite the opposite. Marva was hiding that she bought reproductions and passed them off as originals."

"So, did you know she'd commissioned the Kahlo?"

"She didn't commission it. The original was from a series of watercolors painted in Kahlo's diary. Have you read it?"

Jane nodded. "Yes. Different, for sure."

"One of my buyers wanted more Mexican art, but different. So we talked about it, and he said a Kahlo watercolor was fine; he left it up to me which I'd choose to paint. I painted the one that caught my eye as being both something I could do and do quickly. From her diary. You read it?"

"I did."

"So sad how her leg was amputated after all those surgeries," Queenie said.

"So amazing how she used art to transform her ruined life into beauty," Jane said.

"Anyway, I sold it to him as stock for his shop in New Mexico. From there, I never know where my reproductions go. And I'd never been invited to view Marva's art wall, as she used to call it."

"Did you know about the angel wings Marva was wearing when I found her on the bayou?"

"No!" Queenie's face went white. "The painting

with wings in the diary. It was on the cover too."

"Exactly. Know any other Frida fans?"

"No, just the more casual admirers."

"Same here, except for the new neighbor." She sighed. "I'll let you get back to work."

"I really should."

Jane drove home. Should she report this to Patrice and Jesse? Queenie was not a murderer. She was a painter.

Chapter Sixteen

Jane had pulled Queenie out of the art room ten minutes before class ended. Hazel waved a general goodbye to the handful of artists after class and, as she took the very short walk home, drew her own conclusions about the conversation between Jane and Queenie, all of them upsetting. Surely, Jane had questioned Queenie about Ethan and maybe even her. Nosy bitch.

Maybe, Hazel thought, I can call in a complaint to the police station. Say something like the detective in charge of the murder of Marva has a conflict of interest. Or maybe an anonymous tip would be better. She knew the St. Pete police had an anonymous tip line as journalists advertised the number to call when they reported a serious crime like vandalism or theft. Murder had to be a big one. But what was the number? She'd look it up online. She had to stay under the radar. Hazel did not want anyone to know how much she loathed and despised Jane and her stupid cop boyfriend. They disgusted her with their fresh new romance.

Ethan was setting out the snack they always had before dinner. They didn't call celery with peanut butter or a piece of toast with a cup of tea "lunch." Today Ethan had spread butter on white bread and then added a thin layer of cucumber. The teapot steeped two bags of Earl Grey, which would yield four cups, two each. The cucumber was fresh, the English kind. Hazel kissed Ethan, trying for his lips, but he shifted, and her mouth landed on his ear. She stifled her irritation and a little bit of revulsion as Ethan rubbed his ear, wiping off her kiss.

Don't say anything, she told herself.

"I have cookies, too," Ethan said, setting a plate of shortbread down next to the other things on the kitchen table.

"You went shopping?"

Ethan nodded. "Just picked up a few things. We deserve it after the week we've had."

"We've got trouble." Hazel poured tea. "Jane came to art class today, not to paint, but to pull Queenie aside and speak to her privately. So rude!" She bit into a shortbread and sipped her tea as Ethan composed a response. She wanted his opinion, his assurance that they were in the clear.

He knew it, and he'd give it, after careful consideration. This trait of Ethan's, his careful analysis of all events large and small, was one of the many factors in their marriage that drew them to each other and tightly cemented the relationship. Hazel counted on Ethan in almost every way. He had never let her down, even when he'd been so deeply influenced by Ray that he'd taken up the drinking of bourbon and the ogling of women.

Ethan took his seat across from her. They ate their snack in silence, listening to the rustle of the leafy trees in their yard. It was a soothing sound, somehow alive. Finally, Hazel couldn't stand the silence between them anymore.

"Well, what do you think?" she asked.

"I think we should add something sweet at the end of our snack every day," he said.

"Yes, but what about Jane and Queenie. What were they talking about?"

"Not you and not me."

"No?"

Some minutes went by as Hazel wondered if Ethan planned to answer her question. He ate the leftover cucumber sandwich on her plate.

He got up to clear the dishes, leaving the cookies.

"You didn't like the cucumber?" he asked. She hadn't touched the final two quarters on the serving plate. Then without waiting for a reply, he set the plate next to the sink. "These don't keep well. The bread has a tendency to dry out."

She made no reply.

"Pour us another cup while it's still warm."

By the time Hazel served a second cup of tea, Ethan was again sitting across from her. He sipped his tea. "Ah, good, still warm."

Hazel waited. She had learned to be patient with Ethan. She was never sorry. Soon enough, he delivered a succinct and surprising analysis: He'd noticed Jane's car at the clubhouse and gone over to the library. Thus he'd overheard the conversation Jane and Queenie had had in the hall connecting the rooms. "I wonder," he ended, "if Ray knows Queenie painted that fake Frida?"

"I don't think anybody knows that! Not yet."

"Except us," Ethan said, smiling at his beloved.

Chapter Seventeen

Jane climbed the stairs to the second floor. Dennis lounged on his lawn chair. A pretty mosaic side table held a wine bottle and a single empty glass. The other glass was in Dennis's hand.

"Hi, neighbor!" she said, noting that he'd poured his wine from yet another pricey Chardonnay.

"Hello." He rose from his chair and smiled at her, his eyes twinkling. "Join me, please." He unfolded a second chair. "You and George are the only neighbors I know."

Jane accepted the wine and the seat. She'd think about the murder and Queenie's piece of the puzzle later. "Motive, means, opportunity," Jane said, before she realized she'd spoken aloud. It was the one thing she'd change about herself if she could. Well, and maybe longer legs.

"Main factors in determining suspects in a criminal case," Dennis replied, sipping his wine.

"Yes, damn it." Jane saw the hurt look cross Dennis's face and said, "I'm so sorry. I was thinking out loud. Bad habit."

"Well, I'm just happy I don't check any of those boxes."

"No. It's not you. I just found out that Queenie painted the reproduction you found at the church tag sale. Queenie teaches art classes here. She's lovely. You should meet her. I'll arrange it."

"I'd like that. I think I've seen her work. Does she sign it Q?"

"That's her."

"She's good."

"She'd love to hear that."

"What a huge coincidence. And nobody knew?"

"Nope."

"You saw the police cart off my Kahlo. I have bare walls again."

"Queenie has no motive, no means, and no opportunity. It's a huge coincidence, but she's not a killer." Jane sipped her wine. "There's a large heavy bowl, which was in close proximity to the painting and the scene of the crime. Perhaps Queenie could have lifted the glass bowl and crashed it down on Marva's head with enough force to kill her. But I don't think so."

Dennis leaned forward. "What, then?"

"At first I thought the angel wings were the key to the killer's identity. But now I realize it was the actual key card to the penthouse. Whoever can get in could have committed the crime."

Dennis nodded. "That makes perfect sense. So who has a key?"

"It's not a key. It's a key card that zips them up to the penthouse via elevator. But my guess is Ray, Biffy, Abigail, Hazel…" And not Dennis, since he didn't even know about the elevator key card.

"Why Hazel?"

"She was Marva's best friend. Everyone here gives their best friend a key to their place in case they lock themselves out or lose their own key." Jane remembered how Fred had the key to a condo last time. As the property manager, he had all the keys. Not anymore. "The office has a key to every condo, so that means Bill, the office manager."

"Do you know where Bill keeps the keys?" Dennis said.

"No. Why?"

"Well, just if someone other than Bill knew, they could borrow a key."

"Good point."

"And when I first moved in, I misplaced my key and had to go to Bill for another, since I don't have a best friend here. Yet." He lifted his eyebrows and smiled.

"Come on. Stop teasing. Where does Bill keep the keys?"

"In a safe."

"I wonder who has the combination."

"According to Bill, nobody but him."

"That's a real stretch. I bet that jerk Grant could get into the safe." Jane sipped her wine. Detecting was thirsty work. "I wonder if Marva knew Queenie sold her reproductions to the tourist place in New Mexico?"

"I don't know most of the particulars," Dennis said. "Do you need to call your detective about this discovery?"

"He's the people of St. Pete's detective. And he probably knows."

Dennis sat a bit straighter in his slouchy chair, his eyes alert. Jane wondered how good he was at reading faces. Some people have the knack and others are almost face blind. "So do you and the detective date other people?"

Jane thought back to her recent conversation with Jesse on just this topic. "No, we don't. But neither do we own each other. We only started dating a month ago."

"It's good at our age to be exclusive," Dennis said in a neutral tone.

"Yes." Jane could feel her face color up like a sunburn. Besides the fact that Jesse didn't have time to date multiple women and Jane preferred he didn't, the biggest reason for exclusivity is that neither of them wanted to give the other an STD. At least, that's the way Jane understood it. Maybe Jesse really had no desire to be with another woman. Maybe he only wanted Jane. She reminded herself that he loved her.

Finishing her glass of wine and saying yes to another, just to calm her shaken nerves, Jane sipped. She felt clumsy and out of her depth in this conversation.

"I'm sorry if I embarrassed you," Dennis said. "I wanted to ask you out, but friends is better than nothing."

"Good," Jane said. "My best friend, Kim, has agreed to come out, just the three of us, to the beach for a sunset dinner. I think you'll like her. And Queenie too."

"I'm happy to meet new women. I like the ladies. But not the way I like you."

Jane moved her lawn chair an inch away from Dennis, and wine sloshed in her glass at the abrupt movement. She set the glass on the mosaic table. "I wish you hadn't said that." She wished she hadn't said yes to a second glass of wine. It cost $90 a bottle, and if she didn't drink it, Dennis would pour it out.

"I'm sorry. That was not well done of me. We hardly know each other, but I do like you so much. We have so many things in common, a love of art, good wine, the random tag sale."

Jane laughed. Yes, all true. And he was funny on top of it. She relaxed and said, "I can text Kim to come up right now and have a glass of wine with us."

"Do it!" Dennis said.

So Jane did. Kim brought her own lawn chair and a glass already full of wine.

"Good thing we live next door to each other," Dennis said. "More room for a party."

Jane laughed again. "Right."

She held out her hand for Kim's wine so Kim could unfold her chair. Dennis got up. He shook Kim's outstretched hand before plucking the plastic wine glass, painted with a flamingo, from Jane.

"Wow, glass on the walkway!" Kim said, pointing to Dennis's Waterford stemware after he had introduced himself.

"I have not had the opportunity to buy plastic yet."

"They won't let you into the pool area for happy hour with actual glass," Kim said.

"What time is happy hour?"

"Four o'clock every day of the week," Kim said. "We go on Tuesday." She wagged her index finger in the air between them to indicate Jane and Kim attended this event together. Which was true most of the time. Nobody seemed bothered that at this particular moment they were a few hours ahead of the curve into happy hour.

"You could meet people that way." Jane tried but could not picture Dennis with a plastic wine glass.

"Hmm. Tomorrow's Tuesday, and I thought we were going to the beach for a sunset dinner."

"I'll call and reserve a spot on the upper patio," Kim said, pulling out her phone and calling their favorite new restaurant on the Gulf.

Jane was happy she and Kim had previously discussed where they'd take Dennis on their little tour.

They'd see the pier and downtown, go west to Pass-A-Grill and then north to Treasure Island, ending up at Cook's Fish House. There were four restaurants in the building at the end of the new pier in downtown St. Pete, but for sunsets, Jane and Kim preferred the sea to the bay. It was nice to look out just as the sun melted like a rainbow into water. To see water all the way to the horizon. Downtown, across Tampa Bay, gorgeous as it was, you saw another downtown.

"No problem!" Kim said after speaking briefly and clicking her phone off. "We're in."

Since Dennis already knew about Queenie painting the Kahlo reproduction, Jane's two-glasses-of-wine mind decided it would be fine to tell Kim. She hated keeping secrets from Kim, and really, she never did.

"Oh my gosh!" Kim said, after Jane relayed the story.

"I know! Dennis…well, I was thinking out loud about whether Queenie could be a suspect…"

Kim held up the hand that was not holding her glass of wine. "I know—means, motive, and opportunity." She turned to Dennis and said in a confiding manner, "I love a good cop show." Then she turned to Jane. "What's Jesse going to say about you telling everyone?"

"Just you and Dennis!"

"But Hazel was in class today, wasn't she?"

"Uh, yeah…she didn't hear anything."

"Well, she knows. Maybe Queenie told the class. It's nothing to be ashamed of!"

Just the same, Jane felt sick. Maybe Jesse would be upset. "I'll text him."

"I don't think a text is going to fix this," Kim said.

"You're right." Jane picked up her wineglass and

polished off the delicious final sip.

"Liquid courage!" Dennis exclaimed.

Jane laughed again. Relaxed again. "I'm going inside to phone him, but thanks for the wine, Dennis, and thanks for the sober advice, Kim."

"I'm always on duty," Kim said as Jane plucked her key out of her purse.

"Okay. Dinner is on! Tomorrow before sunset. What time?"

Kim replied she'd made the reservation for five thirty. Jane clicked the lock on her door open.

"Thanks for leaving me a glass of that, Jane," Kim said, holding out her plastic flamingo for the refill Dennis was ready to pour.

Chapter Eighteen

Jane walked down her long hall, satisfied. Dennis and Kim were having a glass of wine alone together. Her next thought was if Jesse would answer her call or if she'd have to type a long text with wine fingers, but Jesse answered on the first ring.

"Hey, Shug."

He must be alone. He sounded beat.

Jane knew he'd work double hard until he caught Marva's murderer. "Where are you?"

"Driving."

Must be work related. She knew not to seek more details. Since the art was bought in another state, the FBI might be involved. Jane could ask Barb about that.

"Patrice with you?" Jane knew Patrice had the day off, but maybe Jesse had called her in.

"No. I'm on my own. What's up?"

"Well, if you're sure you have time to talk…"

"I just got on the causeway to Tampa. So yeah."

The FBI had a field office in Tampa. She'd called Jesse just in time. She'd stick to the facts and not get into details unrelated to the case, like how everybody in Winding Bayou would soon know about the coincidence of Queenie painting the missing Kahlo reproduction. That the painting had been stolen was already all over the news. Journalists were even connecting the missing painting to possible motive for murder.

"Shug?" Jesse said.

She told him everything. About Queenie, about Hazel, and even about how Dennis knew the keys were in a safe. He was silent on the other end until he sighed. "Okay, well, that was quite an assumption on your part."

"I know. Not probable, but I thought, well, it can't hurt to ask."

"She certainly didn't tell us about the painting being her work."

"Well, maybe when you interviewed her, it just didn't occur to her. Marva was one of us, after all. The community was in shock. Also, I guess I forgot to say— I had some wine with Dennis and Kim—Queenie told me she had no idea the 'Kahlo' mentioned in the press was her work. It didn't occur to her that a reproduction of a Kahlo painting she'd sold to a dealer in Taos was the same painting Marva claimed was an original." Jane babbled. "The good news is Dennis and Kim are having a glass of wine together!"

She waited for a word from Jesse. Nothing. A full fifteen seconds crawled by. She had a strong impulse to fill it but resisted.

"Okay, matchmaker sleuth. I think you've done enough for one day."

His tone was neutral again. She liked being called Shug much more than "matchmaker sleuth."

"You still on the causeway?"

"Yes, but not for very long."

He sounded like he was trying to keep his tone neutral, she could hear the strain, but at least he answered her before letting a long silence elapse again. "Talk to you later?"

"Later." Then he disconnected.

Maybe she wasn't cut out to be a cop's girlfriend. Dennis was so much easier. Retired like her. Into visits to art galleries like her. He'd already been to the Dali. It was the first place he'd visited after he'd secured the condo. He'd been to see the Chihuly glass collection, and not because a Chihuly-like bowl had been a murder weapon.

And that was another thing. Jane did not like thinking about murder and murder suspects. If she wasn't dating Jesse, she wouldn't worry so much. She'd never think about it beyond a short clip on the news. Well. It wasn't Jesse's fault that someone she knew in a shared community, not to mention had a glass of wine with, had been murdered.

****

By the next morning, Jane decided Ray had killed Marva. It was always the husband! But she'd dutifully followed the art trail elsewhere, and here's where she'd ended up: in acquiring the art itself, before she died, Marva had done nothing illegal. She just lied. That was a bit shady and made the murder more drawn out than it had to be, pointing in various directions, but it wasn't criminal to lie as long as it was not slanderous or for profit.

Ray probably did not know that the painting was a fake. He attempted to steal it and maybe then he would have sold it, but Marva caught him in the act, and for that, she had to die. Simple. She called Jesse and told him her latest theory, the key angle, which added Bill who had no reason to kill anybody, plus he was too nice. Possibly Grant could have borrowed the key card from the safe. He was chummy with Ray and seemed like a woman-hater, but how would he get the combination?

Sure, Queenie did the painting, which did not make her guilty. "It's a process of elimination."

"Pretty big coincidence," Jesse said, "about the painting."

"I know you hate those."

"If you explain that away…"

"I'd be an FBI agent."

Jesse laughed.

"So I'm sure you've already got Ray at the top of your list." Jane persisted.

"Yes. But the case is considerably weakened without a lick of proof. Unless we get lucky and find a fingerprint on the Frida portrait frame. How likely is that? Would Dennis clean the frame before hanging the picture?"

"He hires people to do those things for him and wouldn't even think of it."

"I hope you're right."

"Did you get a warrant to search Ray's house? His clothing? A copy of the diary, Frida's diary, would be a great find."

"Noted. Also, what do you think I've been doing in all the hours I'm not seeing you?"

Jane didn't have a response for that.

"Tell me at least that Dennis took a shine to Kim," Jesse said.

Jane couldn't lie. "They didn't have a spark. Not like I thought they would."

"Not like you and Dennis have, seeing as you like art and good wine and culture. You're both educated for a life different than mine."

Jane knew it was true, but she didn't want to say that either. "It's *you* I love."

"Love you too, Shug."

"I know it's complicated," Jane admitted.

"I've got a few minutes," Jesse said.

"I really like Dennis. We get each other. We're both retired, so we have time to spend with each other. He makes me laugh. I feel safe with him."

"Does he have a gun?"

"What?"

"I don't think he can protect you like I can, that's all I'm saying. You feel safe with him? His money can't stop bullets. Well, unless he has a bodyguard with a bulletproof vest."

Jane didn't know how to verbalize the ways she felt safe with Dennis. "No bodyguard or vest, but I think being close to a cop, I'm closer to danger."

Jesse let out a big sigh. "Where does this leave us? I just need to know. A minute ago, we were in love. And true to each other."

"I haven't had sex with Dennis!" Jane said.

"Not yet."

"Don't you trust me?"

"I haven't thought much about it, but it's more him I don't trust."

"Do you love me?"

"That I know for sure." Jesse's intake of breath was audible. "See, this is why I hate relationships."

"Why? Because they make you think about things other than your cases?"

"I don't know. You sound a little like my ex-wife. Same complaints."

That hurt. But sometimes Jane's problems with Jesse were like those she'd had with her dead husband. He'd worked all the time too. So, maybe this was love in middle age. It came with baggage. She should tell Jesse. How were they ever going to get closer if they stayed secretive about their feelings?

"And your job, how much you work, reminds me of my dead husband. Did I ever tell you I was in the process of divorcing him when he died?"

"Not that I remember."

"See! That's something I would remember about your ex if you'd told me about her. Hell, I don't even know her name."

"Loretta."

"Oh, of course. Something feminine and pretty, unlike plain Jane."

"Jane. You are beautiful, and I love you. When we're together and I'm not working, I really love hanging out with you."

She had to admit it. He was not like Stan, not in the least.

"Sorry, I'm at my appointment. Gonna have to let you go."

"Okay. Hope you catch a break."

****

Feeling edgy and at loose ends, Jane picked up her sketchbook and drew a murder map showing how the murderer had most likely gotten the body out of the penthouse, dragged by her legs, maybe on a bedsheet, down the elevator and outside by the bayou. The angel wings had to have been with Ray all the way. They would have been either on top of Marva's body or under Ray's arm. He had to have bent the body on the ground so her torso folded forward on her knees. Then he'd laid the wings down and finally lowered her onto them. She thought about taking a photo of the map and texting it to

Jesse, but he had probably figured that out already. Maybe the crime lab people had found something on Ray's clothing. Did they have to check all his stuff? Had Ray brought that big suitcase, the one he packed and took on his way out the door when Marva was still alive, back to the penthouse? Was it possible to have a normal relationship with a police detective? Would he ever retire?

Chapter Nineteen

"I've got an idea about how to get info on Ray." Jane matched her steps to Kim, who walked fast for a short person. "I just need Ethan's help."

Two turtles sunned themselves on a screen contraption floating on the bayou.

"Ask him," Kim said. "I mean, he's Ray's best friend, so he might say no. But Hazel could talk him into it. He loves her to distraction." Kim glanced at the step counter on her wrist.

"Hazel hates me," Jane said.

"No, she doesn't. She's just high strung. And she has this crazy idea that you think Ethan killed Marva."

"Well...not that crazy. Except he has no motive, no means, and no opportunity. Hazel has a key to the penthouse, though, am I right?"

"Yeah, but that doesn't mean she killed her best friend."

"It's just a coincidence then, him out stargazing at the exact time of the murder."

"Yep."

Kim's index finger indicated they should get off the bayou path, walk past the clubhouse, and right out of the complex.

****

After their walk, Jane showered, threw on a cheery red T-shirt dress and her basic black flip-flops, and walked over to Hazel's. Kim had texted that Hazel was fine with Jane popping in. Jane realized she was a little afraid of Hazel. Hazel reminded her of the boy who found her every day when she was eight. He'd come up to her out of nowhere on his bike and say, "I'm going to kick your ass. I'm going to beat you down." He terrorized her, but she'd always run home before he actually did anything. She had been so happy when later that year, he'd moved.

Hazel came to the door and let Jane in, shortbread cookies and iced tea displayed on the coffee table in the living room.

"May I pour you a glass?" Hazel asked.

Jane nodded, trying to figure out why Hazel reminded her of an eight-year-old boy from her childhood. Instead, she told Hazel the bully story as an icebreaker. Her mom always said a good way to make friends was to share a secret. Jane's secret was that she'd been bullied.

"I was bullied too, when I was thirteen," Hazel said. "It was a girl. She demanded I meet her at a certain time and place after school. I decided not to back down. It was silly. I should have just kept dodging her. But we met in a field behind the school. There was a whole circle of girls around us. I planned to punch her in the nose with my right fist and in the stomach with my left. A one-two punch. Ha." Hazel took a sip of iced tea. "I had no idea girls didn't fight like that. The girl pulled my hair and raked her pointy fingernails down my face. She kicked me until I fell, defeated. I hadn't landed one punch. Also all the girls were cheering the bully on. I've never figured it out. What did I ever do to any of them? Nothing!"

Jane nodded. She'd never figured out the boy's motive, either.

"Anyway, when I got home, my mother saw my bloody face and almost fainted. I told her what happened and begged her not to call the principal. That was it. The girl ignored me from then on."

"Bullies are so weird," Jane said. "My mom's a retired psychologist, and she says they get bullied at home by family members, so they pass it on."

Jane placed a cookie on one of Hazel's cute palm tree plates. She wanted a cup of coffee rather than the tea, because in southwest Florida, December was warm but no longer hot. She could have almost worn a sweater. She chewed her cookie and took a small sip of iced tea.

"Would you rather have coffee?" Hazel asked.

"No, this is good," Jane said. She didn't want to put Hazel to more bother. "Where's Ethan?"

"Oh, he's in his office, calculating the next eclipse." Hazel sat next to Jane. "Thanks for believing in him. He'd never hurt a fly."

"He's a good man. You're a lucky woman."

"I am," Hazel said.

Jane decided to plunge ahead. "I'm trying to think of a way to prove Ray killed Marva."

"I know. Kim told me."

"Well, okay, good. I had an idea, if Ethan will agree to it."

"Tell me first," Hazel said.

Jane told her.

Hazel said, "I love it! He'll do it!"

"Are you sure? Shouldn't we ask him?"

"Jane. Ethan has never said no to me. Like never ever."

"All right. I'll see him at the clubhouse tonight." Jane finished her excellent cookie. "Shortbread is my favorite."

"Mine too." Hazel actually smiled at her.

****

Jane wore a camo T-shirt and jacket. She pulled on long jeans because the night was cool and the shrubbery was coarse. Hibiscus grew high enough for her to hide behind, outside the game room window in the clubhouse.

George was waiting for her and laughed when he saw her decked out. "Is that your stalking outfit?"

"Shut up! We are trying to catch a killer here." Jane felt immediately contrite for snapping. "Sorry, George. I'm just nervous."

"Not a problem. Let's book."

"Don't forget to open the window so I can hear Ray."

He flapped his shirt pocket to show her the cigars he had stashed there. "Grant makes a big show of keeping the owners toeing the line, but he breaks all the rules for poker."

It was full dark. Jane let George go on ahead of her. Ethan came out of his place.

"I'm surprised Ethan lets you smoke," Jane said.

"If Ray smokes, Ethan smokes," George replied. "Okay, kiddo, fall back."

Jane went around the tennis courts toward the clubhouse and its side rooms. Outside the card room, dense shrubbery shielded her as she planted herself like a hibiscus and made sure she had a good view as the lights went on and George and Ethan both looked her way.

George opened the window and lit his cigar. He

looked at Jane crouching in the hibiscus leaves and mallow and winked.

"You see anything?" George asked Ethan.

"I don't see anything, George," Ethan confirmed.

Ray came in and smacked Ethan on the back. "Where's your stogie?"

George handed out cigars just as Grant came in. "I canceled the other classes for tonight, so we should be good," Grant said. It was against house rules to play cards for money, but Grant made the rules, therefore he was allowed to break them.

Jane shook in her sturdy boots as the men took their places on the table by the window, lit their cigars, and fanned out the cards Grant dealt. Hazel came in with chips and pretzels, which she sat on the bar. She opened a bottle of bourbon and filled four rock glasses with ice.

"Do you want me to pour, or what?" Hazel asked.

Ray got up and walked toward Hazel, puffing on his cigar. "I got it, hon. You get on home now." Ray splashed liquor in the glasses as Hazel left and said, "Come get yours, guys. I'm not a cocktail waitress."

The men exchanged poker chips for cash. Everybody put in a chip. Jane didn't know how much they were playing for, but she could ask Ethan later. He had not mentioned this part of the game. The money part. Grant stood at the bar, finishing his first drink and pouring a second. He brought it to the table and belatedly threw in a black and white poker chip, same as the other guys.

Everyone had set their cigars in ashtrays as they studied their two cards and then looked twice as long at the four (or was it five, and why did it matter?) cards Grant turned up, one at a time.

Ethan threw his cards down. "I'm out."

George did the same. Ray and Grant kept playing and adding chips to the pile. Finally, Ray called, and they showed their hands. Ray had a full house. Grant had two pair. Jane wasn't sure who won that round. It was supposed to be Ray. The idea was to get him drunk and happy. Instead, he shrugged when Grant gathered all the chips at his side. He did it the way he did everything, with an air of entitlement. He lit his cigar.

Ethan poured another drink. Jane could hear the ice cubes clicking and the glug of liquor as he mixed his drink. It was so quiet, even the bugs were intimidated by Grant. "Anybody else?" He held the bottle up.

George grabbed it and filled his glass. Jane had cramps in her calves. She dared not move.

Ethan brought the bottle to the table.

They drank and smoked and played cards. After his initial win, Grant started losing. He wasn't happy. Ray rubbed Grant's face in all the chips he'd pulled in. Not literally, but…

Come on, guys, Jane thought, feeling the no-see-ums eating alive the exposed flesh at her wrists and neck.

Finally, Ethan said, "Cops find Marva's killer?" to Ray.

Ray was in an expansive mood. "Naw. That guy's in the wind. I figure it was her cousin. Thought since we'd started the divorce, he'd get something out of her. He was too broke to wait for the will, so he tried taking a painting."

"How'd he get in?" Ethan said.

"Hell, I don't know. I wasn't there. She probably let him in."

He puffed away at his cigar, pouring a sloppy drink,

splashing it on Grant's hand as he picked up the cards for a new deal. He didn't seem to be lying. George would know. That's why Jane had Ethan invite him into the most exclusive and illegal card game in the Bayou.

"Watch it, fucker," Grant said, shaking the liquor off his hand.

"What? Your wifey gonna get mad coz you smell like liquor and smoke?"

"Asshole," Grant said. Talk about a sore loser. And he couldn't even accuse Ray of cheating because Grant had been dealing the cards all night.

There were other ways to cheat. She paid attention to the body language, hoping her elusive ESP would kick in. All she knew right then was that Grant wasn't happy and Ray wasn't giving off any guilty vibes. A siren blared in the parking lot, and she jumped clear off the ground. She landed with a distinct rustle against the large hibiscus, her ankle coming down crooked. It hurt, but she was able to keep her mouth shut. Still, it wasn't enough.

"What was that?" Ray said.

Chapter Twenty

"Did you hear a siren? Flip on and off real quick like?" Grant said.

Jane sagged in relief.

"Yeah, I heard it," Ethan said.

"Me, too," George agreed.

"No, over there by the window," Ray said, pointing right at Jane. Ray walked toward the window, but Jane, despite her twisted ankle, had backed out of view. All the way into Jesse, who grabbed her around the waist and pulled her into his vehicle just before Ray came storming out of the clubhouse side door. Jesse hit the siren again, quick on and off, while kissing Jane, completely covering her camo.

"Get a room," Ray yelled and slammed back into the clubhouse.

At first, Jane was too wrapped up in kissing Jesse's lips to notice he was licking her face. Then she wondered how his tongue could be in two places at once, and she froze.

"Stop it, Belle!" Jesse said in a stern tone, pulling a little away from Jane to pet the now-howling dog in the back seat. The howling stopped. "Good girl."

Jane pushed Jesse away so she could turn to the tan and white beagle, who had escaped her cardboard box and was half hanging on the front seat, her doggy toe nails scrabbling for purchase on the upholstery. Jane grabbed Belle's back end and felt a tail wiggling in the palm of her hand. Belle sniffed Jane's arm as Jane scratched the dog between the eyes. Belle let out one last *Ahroo* as Jesse brought her into the front seat.

"This is Belle. She was rejected by the K-9 unit because she has a wheat allergy that didn't show up until she was through her training."

"How did you end up with her?"

"There's a list, but most cops want the shepherds and the Dobermans. So I took her."

"Because nobody else wanted her?" Jane put her hands over Belle's ears. She seemed a sensitive, intelligent dog.

Jesse nodded. He started the car and drove slowly to Jane's condo where he leashed Belle before opening the car door. Belle *was* smart. She was practically dancing by the time she bounded out of the vehicle. Jesse got her to the grass just in time, then stood beaming at the dog like a proud papa as she tinkled. When Belle finished her business, Jesse brought a treat out of his pocket and flipped it to Belle, who caught it in her chops. "Good girl!" Jesse said when Belle had finished her treat. Belle's tail went on another tangent as she looked up at her hero. Jane thought they were both adorable.

Meanwhile, Jane scooted out of the front seat and peeked into the dog-tooth-tattered box. Inside, a chewed-up towel and a bag of organic gluten-free dog food formed a sad pile. Jane left the box and the towel but pulled out the food. Belle spotted the bag of food and began prancing around, clearly excited.

"She loves to eat. And her sense of smell is off the charts."

"Well, let's get her upstairs," Jane said. "I can do

better than that box."

"Oh good," Jesse said.

Jane glanced at Jesse, then down to Belle's chocolate eyes. Belle wagged her tail all the way up the stairs. Once in the condo, Belle went into sniff mode, her nose low to the ground, checking out every corner of Jane's place.

"How are you going to care for a dog during a murder investigation?" Jane whispered.

"Haven't figured that out yet," Jesse said. He sighed and sat on the sofa as Jane arranged large throw pillows on the floor for Belle. "The thing is, Belle was headed for the shelter tomorrow. It's a good shelter, but if she got a cold or anything…well, they can't risk all the animals getting sick."

Jane looked up from where she was helping Belle find a cozy spot on the pillows. "Are you saying…" Jane started but shot a stricken look at Belle and stopped.

"Yes." Jesse made a slicing motion across his neck with his index finger.

"Oh no. That's awful."

"Yeah. I thought I could find a dog walker to come over and play with her, feed her, take her out to the dog park."

Jane stared at Belle, circling around the pillows until she felt satisfied and curled up. Much to her annoyance, Jane's eyes filled. She blinked a few times. Now was not the time to be sentimental. But if not now, then when?

"I've never had a dog." Well, they'd had one when she was a kid, but that was a long time ago and her mom had been in charge of food and whatnot. Jane wasn't sure she should offer to do this.

Jane and Jesse sat, holding hands, gazing at the

sleeping beagle. They didn't say anything for a long time. Then Jesse kissed Jane's cheek. "It's a sweet thought, Shug, but no need."

Belle was darling, but she howled a lot, like now. Her snuggle with the pillows complete, she wanted food and water. And she was not shy about asking for it.

The three of them squeezed into Jane's skinny kitchen. Jane set a place mat on the floor, and Jesse found a plastic container and filled it with water. While Belle was lapping water, Jane brought out her granddaughter Suzy's pink plastic baby bowl and filled it with the kibble Jesse had torn open.

They stood over Belle, watching her eat.

Jane's heart hurt. She missed Suzy and she missed Jesse, somehow even when he was here. She missed her kids, though they were adults with families and lives of their own. Belle would be company. She'd have less time to worry about Jesse or miss her children and grandchild. "I'll take her. At least until the murder is solved."

A beat of silence, except for Belle's crunching, passed.

"Are you sure you're okay with that?" Jesse said. "It's kind of a spur of the moment decision. Girl can't help it if her special food isn't in the budget."

"She's a sweetie," Jane said. "You work all the time, and she looks young."

"Not quite a puppy, fully house trained. Beagles are frisky. And they love to eat. I had to stop and get her food at a vet, and they gave me a recipe for some sort of liver snack so she doesn't eat poop."

"What!"

Belle looked up.

Jane lowered her voice. "It's okay, Belle. Mom and

Dad are just discussing poop."

Belle had finished her food so she and went into the living room, circling her spot on the pillows again. She needed a cute pink collar. And so many other things.

"What is this about eating poop?" Jane whispered to Jesse.

"Beagles love to snack, and if there isn't food, in her case, grain-free food, they'll eat poop." Jesse shrugged like the was no big deal. "You just have to make sure she gets her meals and her treats."

"Whose poop? Her own?" Jane was stuck on this fact. It could be a deal-breaker. Belle eats poop. Belle licks Jane's face. Hell, no.

"This is a dog thing, a beagle thing. They will eat their own poop or the poop of another dog, like in the dog park or wherever they find it. But only if their belly is empty. You gotta keep her topped up."

"She is not a car that guzzles gas. She is a face-licking sweetie who may one day eat poop!"

"She won't if she's fed regularly. She's trained."

Jane looked out in the living room. Here she finally had Jesse. Not a text. Not on the phone. Real live Jesse. And they were having an argument about dog poop. Jesse pulled a sheet of paper out of his pants pocket and handed it to Jane. She looked it over. A recipe for the liver treats without grain, the special food name, a vet name plus contact details, also the name of a pet shelter.

Jesse put his arm around Jane as they watched Belle curl up amidst the pillows.

"I'm not taking her to a shelter. That will be your job." Jane rested her head on Jesse's shoulder. Belle yawned and closed her eyes. "If it comes to that."

"Deal," Jesse said, squeezing Jane closer and kissing

her temple.

"Can you stay?" Jane asked.

"Yes. Patrice is covering for me."

"Anything on Ray?"

"We're following up some leads. By the way, Kim called me about your plan."

Jane felt a stab. "Why?"

"She's worried. It wasn't so long ago she almost got killed by a murderer."

Jane nodded. She got that. Still.

"I was coming over anyway."

"To drop off a dog!"

Jane saw Belle's long tan ear twitch. She was such a smart dog.

"I wasn't planning on just dumping her on you. If you don't like her, I'll take her back."

"No. I-it…I think…she feels right." Jane aimed her phone camera at Belle and clicked.

She posted it to her Facebook. It would cause a sensation among her forty-two friends.

Jesse hugged Jane and kissed her cheek again. Jane turned just a little, and the next kiss had a much more satisfactory landing on her lips. When she came up for air, Jesse said, "Well did you learn anything?"

"Nothing except Ray doesn't act guilty at all, and Grant is a very poor loser."

"Grant? He's the property manager."

"Yeah. He's a grouch anyway, so I steer clear when I see him coming."

Jesse pulled up his phone notebook and scrolled until he found what he was looking for. He was quiet for a while, thinking about whatever, Ray or Grant or some other thing related to the case.

It would be good for her to have Belle. There was a Jesse-sized hole in her life and would be until the murder was solved. She really didn't want to fill it with Dennis. Now she'd be too busy walking her dog and baking liver treats to spend time sipping cocktails and visiting museums with Dennis.

Jesse's stomach rumbled.

Jane laughed. "Hungry?"

"Yes. I'm not going back in tonight. Patrice can handle it."

Jane nodded. Happy she had her sweetie back even if only for one night. "I have soup, salad, and biscuits," Jane said. "Or shrimp and cheese grits. Or both."

Jesse smiled. "I'll take everything. I haven't had a real meal since this started last week. Has it really only been a week? I sure have missed you." He circled his arms around her from behind as she lined up ingredients on the countertop.

"I've missed you, too." Jane wedged the handle of a spoon into the package of refrigerated biscuit dough. With a pop, they inflated out of the package like tiny white pillows. She placed them one by one on a cookie sheet. "Belle will be good company," she said. "I've had quite enough of myself!"

Jesse laughed and went over to the stereo unit. He lifted a vinyl record from her small collection. Jane's dad had a vinyl collection that took up every wall in his office, like a library with albums instead of books.

"White Stripes?" Jesse said.

"That's going back. Perfect. But...won't music wake Belle?"

The dog's nose kicked into gear. She scrambled out of her pillow fort and pranced into the kitchen, her eyes hopeful. And that was before Jesse put the music on the turntable.

Jane set the biscuits in the oven and cued the timer.

"I'll take Belle for a walk and get those treats I told you about out of my car."

"So you can buy them as well as bake them?"

"Yes, but they're pricey. I should buy her food."

"That's nice of you but not necessary."

Jesse didn't reply as he snapped on Belle's leash and walked her to the door. Jane watched a white and tan tail wag, following the wiggle of a puppy butt. She heard the strange sound of doggie nails against the ceramic tile, marching down the long hall.

"Too cute," Jane said, stirring grits into boiling water. Then she defrosted the carrot-ginger soup she'd made weeks ago. She had lettuce and tomato and found a not-too-terrible cucumber in the very back of the crisper. She pulled a block of cheddar out and fed it to her food processer. Got the shrimp rinsing under cold water. She felt warm, so turned on the ceiling fans before draining the shrimp. She opened a bottle of wine just as Jesse and Belle came back into the condo.

"Well, hi, you," Jane said to Belle. "Did you have a good walk?"

Belle seemed calm until you looked at her furiously wagging tail. She gave a quick low bark.

"That's her whisper bark," Jesse said. "She knows she only gets treats when she's on best behavior." He handed Jane the bag of store-bought liver snacks. "You might as well take over. Just ask her to S-I-T."

Jane opened the bag of treats and pulled one out. "Sit, Belle."

Belle immediately sat, her tail still wagging like a

window wiper across the floor. Jane gave her a treat. Belle took it delicately from Jane's fingers. "Good girl."

"She should be set for the night with bathroom. She can have a few more treats, but if you give her more than four or five, you'll wake up to howling at four a.m."

"So she'll be hungry?" Jane asked, fishing out another treat.

"More in need of an urgent meeting with the grass. Bring a plastic bag."

"Okay, so she'll sleep later if I hold off on too many treats at night."

"Maybe until six or seven."

That was fine. At least the sun would be up. Jane poured herself a glass of wine. "Want a beer? Help yourself."

Jesse opened the fridge, reaching for his favorite craft beer. "It's been a week since I had one of these, too," Jesse said, clicking his bottle neck to Jane's glass.

Jane looked around the kitchen, ticking off what she still needed to do to get dinner on the table. "We're just waiting for the biscuits and grits to finish."

Belle paced in a circle around Jane.

"Okay, but just a few more. Sit."

Belle sat. Jane pulled another treat.

"I brought my duffle in when Belle and I came back upstairs," Jesse said.

"Oh good," Jane said. Every single thing she wanted in this moment was right here, in this room.

Chapter Twenty-One

Since she'd become a detective, Patrice had a new office: A big white SUV with white interior. Jesse, as usual, drove. He griped when they had to trade in the black wagon, but this one had the ability to stop on command at Taco Take Out day or night because Jesse said it didn't smell right. They had to break it in. They waited at the Donut Hole's special parking spot for a fresh batch of donuts to be rushed out to them. Jesse wasn't talking. That was fine.

Patrice, as usual, was thinking that the only thing she hated about her job was Tesper's roving hands and how happy she was Jesse liked to drive and brainstorm. Their real office was the SUV.

"Are we sure?" Jesse said.

"Well, we're not sure if it's Ray or Grant, but since Ray's place has been searched and researched, we should look into Grant. He's easy to find, practically lives in his office at Winding Bayou," Patrice explained. "And he loves fresh donuts."

"You're good," Jesse said, "but to catch a killer, you gotta be great."

"Okay, how about the fact that Grant tried to pin the blame on George, Queenie, and Hazel all in one interview? And his wife has been conveniently out of town caring for her sick mother."

"Good. But not motive. We need motive. Evidence

of."

Jesse passed the bag of doughnuts to Patrice, who tucked them into her snack satchel so she could grab the coffees. The new vehicle was beginning to smell like Patrice's favorite hazelnut coffee that Jesse had just passed her. He handed the server a twenty-dollar bill covered by a single because the server would never take the twenty from her favorite cop.

They pulled out and headed to Winding Bayou. "So. Motive?"

"Last time he saw us at the pool, he jumped out of the water and ran to lock his office door."

"Not motive but suspicious behavior. Good job," Jesse said.

Patrice's heart warmed as if blasted by sunshine. So what if her husband had dumped her? So what if her co-worker was crossing some uncomfortable lines? She was a good cop. A good detective, even. She searched thorough the bag for a glazed doughnut.

Jesse sipped his coffee. "So we go in and catch him unawares and see if we can find evidence, whatever it may be."

"Look in corners, but don't be too obvious," Patrice said, nodding. They'd be in the office with the suspect, and they had to pull off a covert search. Lucky for them, Grant had a weakness for doughnuts.

Ten minutes later, fully caffeinated, greasy bag of sugar in hand, they pulled into Winding Bayou. "He's not at the pool. He must be in his office."

Patrice knocked and opened the door at the same time. Grant sat bent over paperwork on an old-fashioned typewriter. She had twenty/twenty vision, but all she saw was that it was a mortgage application. Local bank.

"Moving?" she asked, presenting him with the bag of doughnuts.

Grant pulled the paper out of the typewriter, wadded it up, and threw it in the garbage. "Waste of time," he said, digging into the doughnuts.

"We got jelly for you," Patrice said.

"Where?" Grant kept searching through the bag.

"On the bottom?" Patrice saw Jesse inching toward the wastebasket. Grant stuck his head inside the bag as Jesse bent slightly and pulled out the crumpled paper.

"Napkin?" Patrice covered Jesse's paper rustling by fanning napkins in front of Grant's face. He took one and grunted. Grant inhaled a jelly, then started in on a pecan roll. He ate with his mouth open, grossing Patrice out.

"Don't know nothing new. Been keeping an eye out. Like I always do."

"We're counting on that," Jesse said.

****

"Your turn to drive," Jesse said as they headed toward the vehicle.

Patrice smiled. It was the first time he'd let her drive.

He wanted to study the paperwork.

"Don't forget, he said, 'It doesn't matter,' and he sounded depressed. Just reminding you to have that top of brain while you look over possible evidence," Patrice said.

"Record that in your smarty-pants phone."

"I already did," Patrice said, proving Jesse's jibe.

As soon as they left the gated confines of Winding Bayou, Jesse pulled the crushed paper out of his pocket. In an effort to hide that he was hiding something, he'd kept his hand fisted in his pocket while they talked to

Grant. Patrice knew those wrinkles would drive Jesse crazy. He smoothed and smoothed until she wanted to slap him. A mortgage application? They knew Grant lived in St. Pete proper in one of the smaller historical homes that had not been updated. It was on a main street, and half the houses had been converted to businesses. In that area of the city, most smaller homes had been added to and updated, but with restrictions due to their historic value. A little bungalow could go for a million bucks. Even on a main street. Jesse knew that. No doubt Grant had bought it when they'd been going for peanuts at auction.

"There were three or four of these in the basket. I don't think he'll miss this one." Jesse had finally smoothed out the mortgage application to his satisfaction.

The irritating uncrunching of paper had stopped. "Well?" Patrice asked after she gave Jesse thirty seconds to peruse the document.

"Looks standard to me." Jesse was still reading. "Wait! He's applied before. That property went off the market before he could lock down the deal."

"Does it say what property he was trying to buy?"

"No. He just checked a box. We need the letter from the bank when they informed him the property had gone off the market."

"That's why he was disappointed. He'd lost his dream home."

"Men don't think about houses like that," Jesse said. "He's trying to cash in on the real estate boom in St. Pete."

Patrice stayed silent. She knew Jesse was using his own profile, projecting it onto Grant. Grant was the kind of guy who cared about his environment. Her covert glances around the office had shown guest chairs upholstered in real leather. His desk was sleek and modern, and his computer was top of the line. The floor tiles were not your standard white squares but had fancy turquoise diamond shapes outlined in gold at each corner of every square. Behind him a wall unit neatly hid every piece of paper, any books or mail, even pencils and sharpener. And that typewriter was a manual, not an electric. It would be expensive to hunt down ribbons and carbon paper. Those were tucked away as well. He had a little fridge with a fancy coffee pot on top of it, but no muddy brew burning off from the morning. The machine was buffed and polished until the glass shined. This was a man attuned to his surroundings. Too bad they hadn't done a walk-through of his home, but that was at the time when everything was happening at once and Ray, as the husband, was the main suspect.

While Patrice's mind had been busy creating her own version of Grant's personality, Jesse was on the phone with the bank. She tuned in when she heard him mention the word "penthouse." Patrice once again was left waiting for Jesse. Why didn't he remember to put the phone on speaker? She gestured pressing the button, but he'd already hung up the phone. "Penthouse?"

Chapter Twenty-Two

Jane hadn't seen Jesse since the night he'd brought Belle to her, but he always texted when he got home. So the two of them, dog and Jane, not Jane and Jesse, got into a routine.

For Jane, it meant lots more exercise and fresh air because young dogs like to walk. And walk. Jane had to keep Belle out of the Bayou path because gators had been known to snatch small dogs for snacks, and Belle was a small dog. Soon, walking the condo boulevard and sniffing out all sides and every corner of the four buildings got old, not for Belle, who never came upon a scent she could ignore, but Jane needed new scenery.

Which is why they sauntered into Orange Blossom, the historic neighborhood where families lived in hundred-year-old houses on the other side of the tall condo walls. To get to Orange Blossom, you had to walk out of the condo a block to School Street. Much to explore even there, though the houses were tiny poured-concrete duplexes, from the days when St. Pete had been a resort town and northerners rented by the week. Jane loved the flora, the palm trees so tall, the flowers, even in December, polished with bright dew. The sight and smell of children at recess threw Belle into well-behaved ecstasies.

Once they entered the Old Florida neighborhood, the architecture got way more interesting. Jane had always loved historical homes. The only reason she hadn't bought one was because she'd have no idea how to care for it. Deep into the cobbled streets of Orange Blossom, Jane spotted a house for sale. It looked as if it had been vacant for a while. Jane let Belle lead her up the driveway. Belle was doing that thing where from neck to nose she was an inch from the ground, her concentration utterly focused. As the dog disappeared into the foliage full of overgrown plantings, Jane held tightly to her leash.

Jane wondered if she could peek into the large bay window when Belle let out a long slow howl like none she'd uttered before. Jane tugged the leash, but Belle was determined to stand her ground and let it be known that she'd discovered something. It was what she was trained for, after all. Jane tugged a little harder just in case it was a skunk, and it wasn't dead. Jane had taken Belle to the groomer just yesterday. She still had the pink bow in her hair.

Soon neighbors opened doors and peeped out. Belle had volume to her howls like a good K-9 should. Inch by inch, Jane tugged Belle out of the shrubbery and tucked the dog under her arm. Belle stayed put, but she still howled.

Jane took off a sandal and brushed it over an oleander where it hit something hard. Metal. Jane hit it again as one neighbor came up behind her. Once Belle noted the intruder, she set to barking as Jane uncovered an aqua-colored rust-encrusted copper pipe. She hit it with her shoe. It didn't move. This was one of those horror stories about old houses. The plumbing from 1920 was a nightmare plus a fortune to replace.

The neighbor said, "What is it, pup?"

Jane responded for Belle. "Not sure." She continued to try to find the base of the pipe to see if there was a water leak. "But my dog was trained as a K-9 for the St. Pete police, so in her mind she's doing her job."

The neighbor man laughed.

That's when Jane saw the leg of a body. She hadn't seen the face, but it had to be a woman's body, because the pipe, which Jane followed up the body, emerged neatly from her pelvis. Decay from the corpse filled her nostrils. Jane dropped her shoe and backed up. "Oh God. I think it's a body. Will you call 911?"

The neighbor rushed off on his mission. Jane backed up all the way to the sidewalk. Then she called Jesse.

"Hey, Shug. How're my girls this morning?"

Jane told him the short version. She was just starting to figure out the long version. He said he'd be there in ten. While she waited, she wondered if St. Pete had a serial killer. She looked around at the houses. The faces at the front doors had multiplied. Strong curiosity allowed for robed-and-slippered folk to venture out their front doors. Jane noticed she only had one sandal. Belle started to whine. Jane petted her and whispered, "It's okay, sweetie. The boss will be here soon."

Not just Jesse but a crime scene team arrived. The neighbors had moved from their porches to the sidewalks and were conversing in tight groups.

Jesse squeezed Jane's free hand and rubbed Belle's little head. "You did good, girl." He fed her a biscuit. Patrice parked the car and came over to hug Jane. She noticed the one shoe. And how hard Jane was shaking. "I'm going to get a uniform to run Jane and Belle home," Patrice told Jesse as they watched the police tent go up.

"I'll be over as soon as I can, Shug."

Jane wondered if they had noted the Frida connection. To Frida's life, not any her art. Had she told them that story? She felt numb. Even Belle was trembling in her arms, maybe more from the excitement of the scene. Jane set her down, and Belle relieved herself before hopping into the back seat of a St. Pete police car.

"How many people murdered makes a serial killer?" she asked the officer.

"Three. But it's not just numbers. There has to be similarities. Connections. Maybe the method of killing is the same, maybe the murderer leaves a signature. Like those angel wings at the first scene. Hang on a minute." Another officer approached the vehicle, and Jane's driver got out to speak to him.

So this is only two deaths, Jane thought. But the signature. Jane saw the connection to the most traumatizing and defining episode in Frida's life: the freak accident on a trolley when she was a young woman. Jane rested Belle against her heart. Anyone looking for Frida Kahlo on the internet would soon come upon that story.

It shaped who Frida became as an artist. After the accident, during her many months confined to bed, Frida's father made her a special easel so she could paint lying down. Years later, she eventually painted something that went all the way back to her accident on the trolley in one of her self-portraits. *The Broken Column* was painted after yet another unsuccessful surgery. She never really healed from that tragic accident when she was young. Jane would tell Jesse when he came over for her statement.

Already the tent was up, techs were bustling about,

and the street was alive with beat officers knocking on doors. Jane thought about the details of *The Broken Column* as she waited for her ride. The slit Frida painted down the representation of her upper body showed her spinal column, her lower body covered by a white sheet. Tiny nails protruded from her forehead down her body. White bandages, like a harness, sectioned off her torso into four parts. All Jane had seen of this new body was that an object similar to the trolley rail had gone through her in the same brutal manner as Frida's horrible accident. Frida had lived to paint it. This woman had not lived.

Jane knew much more about the painting, like the fact that originally Frida had been fully nude, but she decided showing her lower half sexualized the painting too much, so she added the sheet. Would that rule out a male suspect? This violence didn't seem like something a woman could do. Didn't they use poison? Weren't most serial killers men?

From Jane's quick view, many differences stood out. Obviously, this actual murder scene sought to re-enact the original accident, but in a clumsy way. Frida's painting showed how she lived in often acute pain for the rest of her life. Her face in the self-portrait is stoic, but there are tears coming out of her eyes.

Patrice came to the car and poked her head into the front passenger window. "Roberts is a good guy." She headed over to a heavy-set cop for a word before disappearing inside the tent. A minute later Jesse texted her, repeating that he'd be over when he could. Her beat-cop driver got back in the car, and they left the scene. No sirens.

Chapter Twenty-Three

The holiday season was no fun with a possible serial killer on the loose. Instead of shopping and eating out at special occasion restaurants, strolling downtown, checking out the lights, and seeing festively themed shows at the theater, Jane, Patrice, and Jesse sat in Jane's condo, stuck on figuring out who the killer might be. Ray had a tight alibi. Could the killer be Grant?

"Is the guy an art lover?" Jesse wondered.

"No," Jane said.

"You sound so sure." Patrice scratched Belle's head.

"Nap time." Jane spoke sweetly to Belle, who yawned, circled her pillowy bed a few times, and flopped.

"Why so sure he's not an art lover, Jane? You trying to give your new art-loving neighbor an alibi?" Jesse's eyes narrowed.

"Of course not! This has nothing to do with Dennis!"

"Okay, okay. Then elucidate your logic."

Jane tried, in the middle of a crime wave, to be in a normal relationship with Jesse. Her marriage had been so abnormal, and she'd blamed Stan, who had never cared enough to be jealous. Was Jesse still jealous of Dennis? What should she do? She had no idea. But she did know why the murderer was not an art lover.

Jesse and Patrice pierced Jane with their cop eyes.

"Well, I've been thinking about it. There's more than one possible reason." She pulled over her book of Frida portraits, found *The Broken Column*, and handed it to Jesse. Patrice stood to peer over Jesse's shoulder.

"First, I don't think a fan of Frida's would use her in this way. It's the opposite of adoration."

"The perp is not a normal fan, Jane," Patrice said.

Jane nodded and shrugged. "My mom's the shrink, not me. But the other thing is the portrait. The first portrait was an almost exact replica of a painting, except Marva was placed beside the bayou. This crime scene today depicts Frida's accident on the trolley, an actual event, something she never painted." Jane pointed at the page in the book on Jesse's lap. "This is a self-portrait of a surgery done many years after the accident. True, that painting is connected, as the surgery which sought to repair the original damage from the trolley rail. But Frida never painted the accident. This was as close as she got."

"So the signature, if that's what you want to call it, doesn't track." Patrice glanced at Jesse, who nodded.

Jane looked confused.

"Serial killers, some of them, the ones who've perfected their crimes, have 'signatures.' Not literally with ink or paint, but one thing they leave behind after each murder," Patrice explained.

Jane nodded. "So this is first-time serial killer."

"Very possibly," Patrice said.

"I think the murderer has no clue about art or Frida," Jane said. "Look at how he threw the reproduction away when he found it was not a fortune in a frame. And now he's telling a story from Frida's life instead of her painting."

"Patrice, question, ah…" Jesse flipped through his

little notebook. "Queenie about that."

Patrice nodded.

Everyone was quiet for a moment. Two. Jane's arms erupted in chills. She didn't want to think about the implication she was about to toss at them. She did it anyway. "This guy has heard me talk about the works or has been studying Frida. Marva's murder was connected to Frida's diary, discovered after her death. I talked about the wings and the accident both."

"Who was there when you talked about Frida?" Jesse asked, pulling out his notebook. Patrice handed him a pencil.

"A group of us were up from the bayou. Patrice, you were there. And Kim. I can't remember who else."

"Okay, Patrice?"

Patrice clicked on her phone and read off a list of the group that had gathered just off the bayou on the morning of Marva's death.

Jane nodded. "Sounds right."

"When did you talk about *The Broken Column*?"

Jane sat and thought for what seemed like a long time. "I don't think I talked about it more than once. I know I told the story at the restaurant, after we saw the Frida exhibit at the Dali." Jane went down the list of names. Jesse tapped into his notepad app while Patrice recorded.

"So there are four names on both lists, aside from you and Marva," Jesse said. "Queenie, Hazel, Barb, and Kim."

"Barb and Kim were at the other end of the table. I don't think they heard the story."

"These murders are not the typical work of a woman," Patrice said.

145

"Thank goodness. I don't want to accuse my friends, who are not in the kind of physical shape to do the work the murders required," Jane said.

"Maybe a partner?" Patrice said.

More silence.

"Maybe," Jesse finally said.

"I'm going dizzy with this stuff. Frida was known for painting two themes. Pain and gender. With the gender thing, she paints herself dressed as a man, her hair slicked back. Or she would often darken her mustache even when dressed as a woman."

"Why would that make you dizzy?"

"Saying the murderer could not be a woman…well, there were times Frida didn't see herself as a woman." Jane paused and sighed. "I think that connection is too tenuous to do anything with."

"It's too far out," Patrice agreed.

"But we have to look at everything. Is the killer sexually fluid? Straight up gay? Was Frida bisexual?" Jesse asked.

Jane said Frida had had both male and female lovers. "But it still doesn't track. Not with our list. We know these women. We'd know if they were lesbian."

"Not if they were in a very tight closet. Remember, except for Barb, they're from a different era well before LGBTQ was mainstream," Jesse said.

"In the media maybe, but lots of people don't like anything gay," Patrice said. "Also, the physical strength just is not there…"

The discussion went on this way for quite some time until Jane said the best possibility was unwitting partners. "Hazel, Kim, Barb, or Queenie told someone, a man, about the so-called fortune in art Marva had and added in the stories. Just for gossip, not for murder. And it's not going to be Barb."

"I know she's your friend, Shug, but…"

"She was also in the FBI and thus is familiar with the idea of keeping your mouth closed when discussing valuables."

"But George used to be a thief."

And so it continued until Belle woke up, shook herself, and stretched before walking into the kitchen.

"She's hungry," Jane said.

"Me, too," Patrice said.

"Want me to order pizza?" Jane asked.

"You two go ahead," Patrice said. "I'm going to eat with my kids."

"Okay, just to cover all the bases, we need to re-interview all four of the women tomorrow morning, Patrice."

Jane walked Patrice to the door, who said, "When he says 'we,' he means 'me.' " But she laughed. "He's got a foot-tall pile of paperwork looking at him tomorrow."

Chapter Twenty-Four

Christmas Day was quiet. Jane and Kim split cooking duties and ate downstairs at Kim's. After pie, Jane's parents called from Seattle, and Marisol allowed Suzy to open her presents on video phone. Kim also got a call, from her granddaughter who'd just had a baby. After swapping baby gossip, Kim asked why Jane had not gone to Seattle.

"I wasn't invited."

"Yikes."

"It's fine. You know how much fun it is having your first great-grandchild. I want my parents to have this time alone with Suzy. They adore Marisol. I'll fly out in the hot months. Seattle summers are lovely."

"Do you always wait for an invitation?"

"No. But Christmas is special."

They touched wine glasses, and the clear chime of crystal rang through the room.

"To special friends!" Kim cheered.

Jane missed Jesse. Working so those with family could be together. Like Patrice. "I wonder what a murderer does on Christmas?"

"Lord knows." Kim shook her head. "When's that next grandbaby due?"

"June!"

"And Jesse will solve the case by then."

"I hope so."

Jane disclosed as much information about the case as she thought discreet. Jesse kept her in the dark, but Patrice had let a few things slip.

"So," Kim said, "you're telling me we know this person?"

"No, I don't know. It could be anyone of you all— not you or Barb, but Hazel or Queenie—anyone they know and gossiped with about Frida."

Kim raised her eyebrows. "My dear, I know you adore Frida, and her stories are sad, thus fascinating, but they are old stories. I don't see Hazel gossiping about Frida."

"I know," Jane said. She also knew Kim didn't want to think the killer was Hazel aided by Ethan. That was one thing Jane had not revealed to Kim, the possibility of a partner. She thought about partners. Hazel and Ethan. Ray and Biffy. Barb and George. Only Queenie didn't have a regular partner. She did, however, have several beaus, as she called them. Also the partners did not have to be real-life partners. Ray and Ethan, for example. Who would Grant's partner be? If the killer was Grant? Someone unknown to the Winding Bayou community?

"If Queenie said something, it was an accident. Too many coco-tinis." Kim had stayed on her own track of thought, and Jane decided not to open up about the partner theory. She was learning just how easy it was for gossip to play hell with a double homicide investigation.

"Yeah." Jane sighed. "Queenie has a hollow leg. And lots of male friends. But what would her motive be?"

Patrice had learned in Queenie's interview, and let drop to Jane, that she'd signed the 1955 date purposely to signal Frida fans that the painting was a repro. So Queenie didn't have a motive. But if she innocently talked about her work on the fake Frida to one of her male companions, which Patrice said Queenie did not admit to, only admitting that she could have let something slip, but her memory when drinking was not good.

"Did Queenie give Patrice a list of her boyfriends?"

"I think they all gave Patrice lists. You did, right?"

"Right," Kim said. "What does Barb think about all this?"

"She's in Michigan with George. But I wonder about that too. I wouldn't be surprised if Barb is doing her own little investigation."

"She's pregnant!"

"She's got George."

"Oh gosh. They could be the crime partners."

"I'd bet my life they are not. But all the more reason they'd be looking for the real killers."

Jane couldn't wait for Christmas to be over.

Chapter Twenty-Five

Jane groaned in pleasure as Jesse massaged her feet. She loved when he did that. It felt like a dream. When Jesse licked her face, she knew it was indeed a dream. Thank heaven she brushed Belle's teeth last night! Jane peeked open an eye as she pushed Belle away from her face. Belle curled up next to her. Snuggles would give Jane a few extra minutes of rest, but she might as well face the day.

She eased herself out of bed, Belle scrambling to jump down too.

"We've got a problem, baby."

"Ahroo?"

"Nothing for you to worry about. Let's get you down to the dog patch."

Belle wagged her tail and stood still for the leash to be attached. She'd chased a squirrel the other day and Jane had scratched her legs up hunting through the bramble along the bayou. It was well known gators loved little dogs.

"Okay, let's go, so we can come back up here and Mama can have her coffee."

Jane's phone rang on the way back up to the condo. Her mom.

"Hey, Mom. How's everybody in Seattle?"

"Well, we were good until Marisol looked up the local news from St. Pete on her tablet."

"What?" Jane held her breath.

"You've got a possible serial killer in your backyard. We're worried. Don't worry, we'll be back in Florida by the time Jesse finds out who killed Marva and the other person. Who is the other person?"

"The police have not released a name, but Patrice told me she had nothing to do with anybody in Winding Bayou. She lived in Orange Blossom." She didn't add that the poor woman had been found outside her home, in the shrubbery, killed in the manner of Frida's trolley accident. It was too bizarre to explain without coffee.

Just as she hung up with her mom, many promises of being careful later, her phone rang again. Barb. Jane wrangled Belle's breakfast and said hello. She flipped the switch on the coffee pot, silently thanking Jesse for preparing the pot.

"How was your Christmas?" Jane asked.

"Just wonderful," Barb said with a thick layer of irony. "Wonderfully cold, that is."

"When are you coming home?" Jane took that first sip of coffee, and it righted her world.

"Soon as we can," Barb said. "There's a baby shower for my back to endure first. But meanwhile I got that name. The second victim."

"Oh my gosh, does Jesse know?"

"Guy doesn't answer his phone. So I don't know. She owned a home, we have her address, it was easy," Barb said.

Jane sat with her coffee, ruffling Belle's hair when she finished her food and curled next to her for a nap. "So, the name. Loni Andresson."

"Fake?"

"You're a genius, honey."

"But why would she want to call attention to herself like that if she had an enemy?"

"She wouldn't. Thus, she had no known enemy."

George yelled in the background. "Everyone's in Aspen."

Jane's face crunched in puzzlement. "What's he talking about?"

"He means," Barb said, "his studio people. He's been asking around about Loni Andresson."

"But there's nobody to ask," George yelled.

"I don't think she's an actor," Barb said. "Well, thanks for the heads up. Are you going to leave Jesse a text?"

"No, you're right, her name was easy to find. I assume he knows by now."

"Where's your new neighbor?" Barb referred to Dennis.

"He's been hanging out with Rusty."

"Another possible partnership," Barb said.

"Sweet as pie. Rusty and Dennis are keeping their distance, though."

"Why?"

"I don't know," Jane said. "He hardly says hi when he's with her. And she cuts me dead." Jane's face dropped when she took a sip and realized her coffee cup was empty.

"Rusty, huh?" George said.

"Dennis did have the painting, and he thought he was buying the penthouse. Those two things can't be overlooked," Barb said.

When Jane liked someone, she tended to cross them off her list of suspects. And she liked Dennis.

"Could Loni Andresson be the unknown friend of

153

Queenie?" Barb said.

"Possible. Patrice has a long list."

"How is Patrice?" Barb asked.

"She's great. Over her dirtbag husband. Parents moved in, and so she can do her job without worry."

"Think she'd talk to me?"

"Probably not in an official way. I usually meet her for steak and martinis when she lets any info slip."

"Now that we bought that house in Lemon Gem, we could have her at the housewarming. I'll barbecue steaks and make sure there's plenty of gin," George said.

"Vodka," Jane said.

"Jesse still working hell hours?" George said.

"Yes." Jane pouted. "New house?"

"Good," George said. "Then he won't come."

"George!" Barb said.

"Kidding!" George said. "Jane, you know we been talking about a neighborhood with kids and a good school for the little one. We found something."

Jane felt a zap in her heart. She ignored it. People moved on. Still, George had been her closest friend next to Kim when she'd moved into Winding Bayou. But Lemon Gem wasn't far. She tried letting it go again.

"You can walk over with Belle," Barb consoled. "Meanwhile, we're not moving until February."

Chapter Twenty-Six

Belle needed to go out. Jane leashed her up. Maybe she should move. Get a place with a yard and a fence for Belle. Winding Bayou was spooky. Even Santa couldn't cheer this place up. Also it wouldn't be the same without George and Barb. She stopped brooding when Dennis came out of his front door, tennis racket in hand, no Rusty in sight.

"Good pooch," Dennis said, petting Belle while twisting his neck to look toward Rusty's condo and swiveling back to Jane when he saw all was clear. Jane couldn't figure it out. Why was Dennis acting so nervous about Rusty? And what did he see in her? Yes, her cats were cute, but she wasn't. For one thing, Rusty was as old as Barb and George put together. And she had not aged well.

"She was napping when I went down to say hi to Barb and George."

"Oh, they back?"

"Yeah. Not for long. They bought a house. Moving in February."

"Hmm." Dennis waved his racket at her. "Can't be late."

After Jane and Belle returned from their walk, Kim called. "I know I said nobody would gossip about Frida, but I've been rethinking. People gossip about anything," Kim said. "It would start with the murders. Then someone would add the Frida parts, just to show off. Then more people would hear and the gossip would spread. I hate to think it's Queenie."

Jane hated to think that too.

****

New Year's Eve and still no break in the case. Nothing the police were telling the public, including Jane. The newspapers reported Tampa's FBI field office had been called in for help. Jesse pretended he didn't care, but she knew he took it personally when he couldn't quickly solve a murder without backup from the Feds.

"Shug, you got a lint brush?"

Jane found one under the bathroom sink. She handed the brush to Jesse. The swank blue crystal bracelet he'd belatedly given her as a Christmas present when he'd arrived sparkled on her wrist. He wore the watch she'd given him. They'd laughed that they'd both bought wrist gifts. Jane thought it linked them, but in a more romantic way than handcuffs. Jesse looked so fine in his tuxedo. They were undercover, but everybody knew Jesse was lead detective on the serial killer case and they knew Jane sometimes helped, especially when a case involved art, as this one did.

"Zip my dress, please." She turned her back toward him. He kissed her neck as he zipped her up.

"By a minute past midnight, if we haven't heard anything, we leave the party," Jesse said.

"Fine. I haven't stayed up past midnight in years."

"I see you have your dancing shoes on."

Jane glanced down at her feet. Silver and gold sandals. They were so comfortable she'd bought a dress to match.

"Did Kim make sure our table includes Queenie and

her date?"

"Of course. Plus Hazel and Ethan, Ray and Biffy, Kim and Fred, and us."

"Fred, huh?"

"Just friends."

****

A banner across the clubhouse stage sparkled out the new year: 2020. The disco ball whirled. A pianist played soft ballads, cocktails were consumed, the appetizer buffet did a brisk business. Hazel led the social committee, and Jane smiled as she whisked by.

Hazel stopped in her tracks. "Jane," she said, and hugged her.

Jane tentatively hugged her back. Maybe Hazel was on meds or something, because she had really chilled out from the bitch she'd been just weeks ago.

"What a great job," Jane said, breaking the hug first. "Everything looks so lovely." The tables were covered with white linen, ready for the sit-down steak and lobster dinner. The band started at seven thirty, and there was a cheeseburger buffet half past midnight. By which time Jane hoped to be in bed with Jesse.

Jane joined Jesse and Ray at the bar where Jesse nursed a ginger ale as Ray pounded down scotch. "Where's Biffy?"

"How the hell should I know?" Ray said, his face turning a darker shade of his usual ruddy. "She's supposed to be here by now."

"Still getting ready?" Jane guessed.

"Women." Ray shot a look at Jesse. "Am I right?"

"I like women," Jesse said. "Especially Jane."

"Huh." Ray continued to drink.

All eyes swiveled to the front doors when Biffy

walked in wearing a dress cut to her navel. Ray brightened considerably. "Here comes my girl," he said as Ethan wandered up and pretended to leer.

"She's a looker for sure, Ray," Ethan said.

Jane was glad Hazel was busy elsewhere.

"Thanks. Got her hair and nails done. Got a spray tan. Got a new dress and necklace." Nobody could fail to see the sparkler that plunged with her neckline. "Got perfume and a massage," he bragged.

"Hazel looks beautiful, too, Ethan," Jane said. When you had a girlfriend twenty-five years younger than every other lady at the ball, of course all eyes would be on her. All male eyes. Except Jesse's. He was checking out Queenie's date as they walked up to the little group that had formed around Ray and Biffy.

Jane and Jesse squeezed hands.

Queenie's date was nobody they knew, but Jane had heard about him from Patrice. A retired FBI agent, working as a P.I. Did Queenie know? Certainly by the squeeze he gave her hand, Jesse knew. About eighty with jet black hair. The number of men who dyed their hair in Florida amazed Jane.

Jane and Queenie talked about the new show coming up at the Dali in a few months. The museum had the world's largest personal collection of Dali's works, donated by local patrons of the arts who had been early and loyal collectors of the artist. The museum also displayed a number of works by rotating artists related artistically to Dali in a smaller annex. That was where the Frida show had been featured.

"If Marva was here, she'd say the name of her dress designer," Kim whispered to Jane and Queenie.

"I've never been a fashionista," Jane said.

"Too expensive," Queenie added.

"I could not tell a real Chanel from a fake," Jane said. She could have smacked herself as soon as it came out of her mouth. "No offense, honey. I meant a purse. Or a jacket. Your reproductions are gorgeous. I've been checking you out online. You do a better Picasso than Picasso."

"Thanks, dear, but no worries. It pays the bills, and it's fun," Queenie said. Her mouth pursed when she saw Jesse had her date pinned to the bar. She went over and broke things up by introducing Drake to everyone. He even sounded like a 1950s investigator. Wasn't that what Paul Drake did for Perry Mason? Investigate? Who in the world could his client be? Not Queenie!

"I hear you've got a second victim," Drake said. "A woman."

"No comment," Jesse said, while Drake asked for a bottle of champagne.

Queenie handed the bartender a bowl of strawberries, the height of elegance when dropped in a coupe of champagne, Jane supposed. Then she scolded herself. She had no call to judge an artist who makes a living painting a few reproductions every year. A widow of seventy-five who still managed to have a very active love life.

Drake handed Queenie her champagne with the strawberry garnish. "Anyone else? Ladies?"

Jane craned her neck. Prosecco. Not Brut champagne, Jane's favorite, but an acceptable substitute. Drake was making an effort.

"Sure," Jane said.

Kim appeared and asked for one as well. "I escaped from Hazel. She's a taskmaster!" Kim wore a darling dusty-pink dress with a crystal collar.

Everyone laughed, including Ethan. "Gotta love a worker," Ethan said.

What did it take to make a successful marriage? Be the 1950s housewife, cater to your husband. Bring home the organic turkey bacon and cook it, too. Ethan kissed his wife, who looked dreamy-eyed. Also keep romance alive. That takes two, and as her mother had often told her, Stan had never done his part after the kids were born. That was the other thing, be a stay-at-home mom. Have cookies and milk ready when the kids came home from school. She had missed out on so much by working. Her mom had started working when Jane was twelve or thirteen. Old enough to stay home on her own. What else for the perfect wife? Be beautiful. Make it seem effortless. Dress impeccably. Greet hubby with a martini when he came home from his hard day of work, even though you had three jobs—house, kids, and career. That's what made a happy marriage. That's why she couldn't do it. She'd tried.

"Where'd ya go, Shug?" Jesse put his arm around her and squeezed.

"Jesse here was just saying he couldn't talk about the murders, but isn't that what everyone else is gossiping about?" Drake said. "Sorry, detective. I know the rules. Shutting mouth now. Except to drink!" And he drank half a beer from the bottle before he came up for air and kissed Queenie.

Jane could tell by the tone of Jesse's voice he knew Drake was former FBI, too. Well, it was Jesse's job. He'd know every private detective and FBI agent in town on sight.

Later, Jane and Jesse found a quiet corner (half of

the club emptied out after dinner when the rock 'n' roll band came on) and she said, "So he's dating Queenie, because he's following the same lead as we are?"

"Yes. Maybe. I'll sort it out. Let's dance."

Chapter Twenty-Seven

Jane's mom and dad arrived from Seattle January 3. They smelled like Suzy. Maybe because they'd babysat for Suzy so Marisol and Doug could go out with their friends for New Year's Eve. Mom checked in the minute they landed at the little St. Pete airport, and Jane took off to taxi them home. She'd missed her mom more than usual for a particular reason.

Jane dusted, vacuumed, and cooked chili for her folks while they unpacked and napped. She knew they had all the ingredients on hand and knew her parents' pantry like her own, right down to the spice shelves.

She had not seen Jesse since New Year's Eve. It had been a nice night. He was a good boyfriend, but then she was doing almost all the emotional work in the relationship: making sure they stayed in touch, assuring Jesse she loved him even though he could not tell her what he was doing or when he'd see her next, sending cute captioned texts of Belle, but not too often. How often was too often?

Jane's mom looked refreshed when she joined her in the kitchen. "It's good to see you, honey. That chili smells lovely."

"Cumin. Your recipe. I know it by heart. Made macaroni for Dad to mix in and found oyster crackers in the pantry too. I missed you both so much."

"I would have never left if I thought Jesse would be

wrapped up in another murder."

"It comes with the job," Jane said it with more spirit than she felt. "And oh, it was great to see Suzy and you together."

"But why didn't you just come with us?"

"I got the strong sense that Marisol didn't want me there," Jane said. "And Danny's working like crazy on Wall Street plus pampering a pregnant wife, so he wasn't there either."

"The two of us should go to New York and see your brother."

"Before the baby shower?"

"Oh…I forgot. That's in March, am I right?"

"Yes, and we have our tickets."

"Okay, well, what else is new? Everything okay with you and Jesse?"

"I guess. Tough to tell when I hardly see him." Jane never hid any of her emotional turmoil from her mother. She'd always counted on the former psychiatrist to ground her.

Jane's mom nodded. "How's Belle?"

"She's good. Kim has her. She refers to herself as 'Auntie Kim.' "

They laughed, but Jane's heart wasn't in it.

Her mom sensed it. "What else?"

"Just feeling insecure."

"About Jesse?"

"Bingo."

"I think that's natural. It's a new relationship. Build slowly. Don't jump into intimacy."

"I would if I could, but his job makes it impossible!"

"Maybe that's a good thing. How can I help?"

"Okay, well, Belle, just as an example. How often is

too often to send photos?"

"Depends. You know he's really busy at work right now, so not when he's on the job. Or sleeping." Her mom was never at a loss for good advice, and Jane appreciated it.

"Yeah, and that's about all the hours in the day. I've been sending him one early in the morning when I know he's making his protein drink and scrambled eggs."

"That doesn't seem excessive to me."

"And sometimes one at night, after he texts me that he's home and heading for bed. I put the one in the morning with just Belle, and then sometimes at night I send one of both of us."

"Okay, well, maybe that's a good limit. Does he respond?"

"Always a heart emoji."

"Would be nice to have a conversation, even a text conversation." Her mom reached out and rubbed Jane's arm.

"I wish. He has not one minute to talk to me."

"What about Patrice?"

"Well, yeah, but after she's done working the case, he's got paperwork and she goes home to her family." Jane bit her lip, surprised at the swelling of tears in her eyes.

"Oh, honey, come here." Her mom hugged her tight. "You two will be fine. I have a good feeling about this guy."

"I thought I smelled chili!" Jane's dad said, coming out of the bedroom wearing sweatpants, his hair sticking up like a punk rocker.

"I knew it would be cold today," Jane said, glad for her long-sleeved tee and matching cotton pants. Even in

Florida, it got cold in winter.

Dad lit the fire. "You don't know cold until you've been to Seattle in winter. At least there was no snow, but Suzy really wanted it. Kid actually prayed. On her knees. Every night. For snow." Dad laughed as he got out three bowls and opened the bag of oyster crackers.

****

Jane felt so much better driving home from sharing a meal and lots of love with her parents. She knew what Barb had talked about now, why she left the FBI and craved a normal family life. Jane had had that as a child but never as a parent. Well, maybe for a minute. When she and Stan were first married and having babies? She knew he'd loved her, she remembered he'd bought her a bouquet of flowers when Danny was born. When did that change?

It was time to change her thoughts and look at what she had now. Friends. A grandchild. Grown children doing well. But did she have Jesse? Would she ever have a normal family with him? Jane had read that the number one reason for happiness in older years was a loving relationship. A good marriage. Okay, well, she and Jesse were not there yet. They'd only been dating since Thanksgiving. It was unreasonable of her to think they'd be any closer than they were. But she knew for sure Jesse was nothing like Stan. She pulled into her garage and went to grab the mail.

Someone came up behind her. She sensed it. She heard it. But lots of people came to get mail this time of day. Kim was probably on her way. Then she saw stars. She'd been hit from behind.

Then Kim screamed and yelled, "Stop! Murderer!"

Oh, good, Kim was here. Then Jane's world went away.

Chapter Twenty-Eight

Jane woke up in the hospital. Patrice and Kim were there. So were her parents. The bright light made her feel like she was heading toward heaven. Was this a dream?

"Kim." Jane groaned. It hurt to talk. "You saved my life."

"Damn straight," Kim said. Kim, who never swore, cursed.

"Honey, oh, thank stars you're okay," her mom said.

Her dad was crying. Patrice was on her phone.

"I saw stars. Now there's the light." Jane pointed up. "My head hurts." She sounded looney, even to herself.

A nurse bustled in and adjusted something coming out of her arm. A morphine drip. Soon, Jane felt better. The nurse was clearing the room. Only Patrice stayed. She clicked off her phone and jammed it into her pocket. "He's on his way."

"Jesse?"

"Yes, ma'am."

"Where's Belle?"

"With George and Barb."

"How long have I been here?"

"Two days."

"Did they catch the guy?"

"No. He was masked, full face. Kim called us, but she said he ran and jumped over the fence to Orange Blossom 'like a ninja.' Her exact words. By the time we got there, no trace. It's like his shoes, size eleven sneakers, ran through the brush for two or three steps—"

"Three steps." Jesse's voice.

Jane's brain wasn't working right. Where was he? Oh. Her eyes had closed. She opened them and tried to smile. Her smile wasn't working right either. Everything felt crooked.

"How you feelin', Shug?"

"Dandy." Where had that word come from? Somewhere deep. She'd never said it before, but her grandpa used to say it all the time, for a number of reasons. She saw him so clearly in her messy brain. "Tired." Her eye lids floated down, but she was still awake. Aware. Jesse was asking her to look at something, but her eyes were too heavy.

"Can you hear me, Shug?"

She tried to nod, but her head hurt. How could that be when the nurse just gave her a gallon of morphine? She let the clouds take her away. It would all be okay. Jesse was here.

****

When she woke up, a day or an hour later, Jesse was still there. This was unfathomable to her. Jesse never stayed.

"Shug. Just rest. I'm not leaving. I have something to ask you about. But can you talk? Don't push yourself. You got hit pretty hard. There was some bleeding, but it's better now."

"Internal or external?" She lifted her hand to the bandage wrapped around her head.

"Both, but when you tried to move your head, that is the first time you moved in three days."

"Three days, three steps, three-three-three. Am I going to be normal again?"

"You're getting better by the minute, Ms. Chasen."

Oh. A doctor was here.

"No stitches, the swelling is under the skin. Just you take it easy for a while."

"I don't feel like doing much," Jane admitted.

"That's a good thing. You are getting better, though. Your speech has improved. You moved your arm to touch your head. Can you lift your other arm?"

Jane lifted. A nurse appeared at her feet and picked her with a needle. "Ow," Jane said and made a feeble attempt to kick the needle and the nurse's hand away.

The doctor put his hand on her legs, moving his fingers over first one, then the other. "You feel that?"

"Yes, but my boyfriend's here!"

Jesse laughed. "It's okay, Shug."

****

The next day she managed to keep both blurry eyes open for more than ten minutes. Her thoughts were ironing out. She'd been getting the mail. "He called me a bitch!" Jane said. "Right before he hit me. Really hard."

Jesse nodded. "Hammer." He put his hand to his mouth, then switched it to his pocket. His eyes caught hers. "You scared me to death, Shug. We just found each other, and for a minute, it looked like I was gonna lose you."

"I won't let you go. Not ever. Not even for a million dollars," Jane said. She knew it was probably too much, but Jesse grinned and took her hand. The one with the IV in it.

"A million, huh?"

"A billion," she said.

"Yes, good, because a million ain't what it used to be."

She laughed. For some reason, her head hurt when she laughed, but it didn't hurt so bad today. "Did you mention a picture? Guy left it at the scene? Or was that a dream? I can look at it now."

Jesse handed her an eight by ten of herself, blown up from a polaroid. It was from a long time ago. From college, when she's studied for her MFA. There was a typed caption, *Jane as Frida*, centered at the bottom of the photograph.

"Where the heck did you find this?" She wanted to laugh, but she was also afraid. "This was a fun girls' day. My friend Patsy—lawsy, she's dead now twenty-five years—she took it. She gave me those pants when she lost weight from the cancer. I would never buy pink-and-red-striped pants."

"So this is you?"

"Course it is."

"Well, I had to be sure. There is a picture of Frida's head you're holding up there. Can't see your face at all."

"Yeah. That's from Deb's calendar. We were just goofing."

"So this picture is more than twenty years old?"

"Well, Patsy was alive, so yeah. And that's Deb's house in Detroit before she moved to St. Clair Shores. I remember how she used those yards of chiffon as a valance."

Patrice came in with her recorder going. Jesse recapped what Jane had just told him. He didn't take out his phone.

Patrice kissed her cheek. "So this picture is from last

century?" Patrice said.

"Yeah," Jane said. "I think 1990-something. Patsy died in the 90s. I think 1995."

"Spell her last name for me," Jesse said.

Jane found she could not spell. "Call my mom. She knew Patsy."

The room dimmed, and Jane heard Patrice say "will do" as she faded. Patsy. Patrice. She was lucky to know them both. If she died from this head wound, would she see Patsy again? Compensation for never seeing Patrice or...

Jane heard no more.

Chapter Twenty-Nine

Ethan went to his poker club again, and Hazel brought over snacks to the bar as she always did. The men didn't notice her; she was a piece of old furniture. This steamed her because Ethan was turning into one of them. It was bad enough when he started hanging with Ray and then the boob thing, but at least she'd had Marva. She really hated Grant who was talking about Jane and calling her a bitch and saying it was good that someone had knocked some sense into her.

If Hazel hadn't been so afraid, so suddenly, she would have told him off. Jane was not so bad once you got to know her. And Grant was a fake king, Winding Bayou his fake kingdom. At the New Year's Eve dance he'd pranced like a prom queen, doing spins and things, clearing the floor with his sheer audacity in claiming the room by dancing all over the place. He'd knocked the line dancing ladies off their stride so many times they gave up and went home. Hazel wasn't the only one who hated him.

Hazel left the bar deep inside the clubhouse and called Kim. "You got that Patrice's number? She gave it to me, but I lost it."

"I got it," Kim said. "What's going on?"

It was dark out, and Hazel was almost to her door. She looked around. Nobody was following her, but Hammer Man might be out there somewhere melting into the shrubbery. "I'm coming over."

"Are you sure? Grant put out that bullet alert that we should stay in after dark."

Once Hazel crossed the boulevard, she breathed easier. "He's not the police." She stepped up her pace until she walked the path to Kim's door. "I'm almost at your door."

Kim's condo was lit from within, creating that cozy feeling of safety. Hazel saw her at the door. "Thank you," Hazel said, finally stepping over the threshold. Hazel was not a huggy person, but she hugged Kim.

Kim grabbed Hazel by the arms, gently pulling out of the out-of-character hug, and said, "What!"

"Can you just call her?"

"Already did. She'll be here in a few minutes. She's been at the hospital, but it's almost time for Jesse to relieve her."

"How's Jane doing?" Hazel startled herself. Kim's sweetness was rubbing off on her just like Marva's malevolence had done once upon a time.

"One step forward, two steps back." Kim looked about ready to cry. "That bastard almost killed her. As it is, she may never be the same."

Patrice rapped on the door, and Kim waved her in.

"Let's get out of this room, or could you pull the drapes?" Hazel said.

They went into the living room. Kim had a pot of coffee, cups, sugar bowl, and creamer. Her wedding set, Hazel realized. Only used for special occasions. She'd also locked the door and closed the curtains. They were an inner circle with a policewoman detective here to protect them. Jane wasn't the only one who needed a guard.

Hazel was too tense to notice Patrice recording the conversation. If she could help, she would. She told her story. "And then he said 'bitch deserved it'!"

Kim poured her a coffee, and even though she didn't think her hands were shaking, she spilled some on the way to her mouth. Hazel had come into the mail room right after Kim had scared the guy away. Kim had seen him clobber Jane with a ball-peen hammer. Now everyone was calling the guy Hammer Man.

"Oh Kim, I'm so sorry," Hazel said about the spilled coffee.

"No, no, no. You sit. I got this. You poor thing," Patrice said.

"No, you two sit."

Kim jumped up and disappeared into the kitchen, and Hazel was alone with Patrice. "I'm scared," she said.

"Tell me about it. Hammer Man—don't tell Jesse I'm calling him that, it's unprofessional—has got us all on edge."

"But Jane's going to be all right?"

Patrice's mouth set itself in a tight grim line. "I think so."

The words she said didn't match the look on her face. Well, Hazel knew she and Kim would survive.

Chapter Thirty

Jane was sick of being sick. In the hospital instead of home. Those flashes of fuzzy thinking. The way the world tilted if she moved too fast, even lying down on a bed. Her doctors, too many to remember their names, assured her the surgery had gone well, the brain bleed had been…taped? Did they really say taped? She didn't care, focused instead on "the surgery had gone well."

A doctor came in like she'd conjured him.

"Hey," she said. "Am I going to die?"

"Not today. Not from the injuries that brought you here. But everybody dies."

Bedside manner, not so great. She wondered if he was considering moving her to a psych ward.

"Yeah, I know." She lifted both her arms at once and stretched hoping to impress with her muscle coordination. "I'm just bored. Want to go home. My dog needs me."

She searched her brain file to come up with the dog's name. Belle. How could she forget Belle for one second? She felt deep shame, but then reminded herself she'd been hit hard on the head with a hammer.

"What's its name?"

"Belle." She wouldn't say anything about the way the doctor called Belle an "it." There had been one or two flashes of anger on Jane's part that had gone on her chart. Nurses. Doctors. She wanted out. Now! At least she knew not to say it out loud. At least she knew not to scream. She was not afraid of Hammer Man. Kim had said that was the name the news had been calling him. The news made a big deal that the serial killer didn't finish his job. Well, damn it, he never would. If she could get out of here, she's figure out who the hell he was.

Was it Dennis and Rusty? Dennis had sent flowers. Rusty's name wasn't on the card. Jane had never known her well. The doctor hovered. She didn't want to know him. She wanted to be away from them all.

The doctor left, and Patrice came back in. That was nice. Someone was always with her. Even sometimes Jesse. But Patrice was nice, too.

"What day, approximately, do you think they'll release me? I can walk to the bathroom and use it too. I miss my bidet! Hell, I walk the halls. I'm off morphine."

"I'll find out," Patrice said. "Did you recognize the voice yet?"

No. She shook her head instead of answering aloud. The fact was that damn voice was getting fainter and fainter. At first she'd forgotten he'd even said anything. Then she remembered and was sure she'd heard it before. But when? And who was it? A man. Hammer Man. She shuddered.

"You want your bed jacket?"

It was not an actual bed jacket, but a loosely knitted peach sweater two sizes too big. Jane told Kim where to find it, and Kim found a police escort and discovered the sweater at the bottom of a drawer and brought it to the hospital. It was Jane's comfort sweater and had been even before she'd moved to Florida.

"Any chance Kim's police escort could turn into something?"

Patrice laughed. "He's practically a teenager."

"That wouldn't bother Kim. She's not agist. Is that a word?"

Patrice laughed.

Jane enjoyed people laughing at her jokes, but these days they laughed even when she wasn't joking. They laughed in a way that Jane knew meant they thought she was kidding around. And she wasn't. Kim needed someone now that Dennis was making time with Cat Lady. Er, what was her name? Rusty.

"What's new on the case?"

"Not a damn thing," Patrice said.

"I was thinking, if there were only three footprints, maybe he jumped the fence again into Winding Bayou."

"Yeah, we think that too," Patrice said.

"I'm glad Barb and George are moving. It's not safe there."

"It will be when we catch him. He's lying low. Or they. We still think it's a team. The FBI did a profile, and they think so too."

"Hmmm. It's got to be someone everyone knows. Someone everyone's used to seeing around all the time. Maybe not lying low, just plotting. Did the FBI check my devices?"

"Yep. That picture is not on your laptop, your phone, or your iPad."

"It's older than all the tech combined. That's why." Jane pondered. "Did I tell you about the black box of photos?"

"Yes. You have a lot of photos. Still checking for prints."

"Did I tell you about my photo albums?" Jane wasn't sure, but she might have forgotten about the albums.

"We found them. On a shelf in your bedroom, right?"

"Yes."

"And a book maybe thirty years old, early 90s, has a photo missing from a set of party photos. A girl's get-together, just like you said. Your captions and journaling have really helped with that."

"Oh! Who would have thought a hobby would help with a murder case?" Jane said.

"I know, but it happens more than you'd imagine."

"All those years. Where did they go?" Jane remembered Jesse, how he liked to say "Where'd you go, Jane?" when she went silent for a while.

"Is Jesse coming?"

"You tired of me already?" Patrice said.

"No. I just wondered."

Patrice patted Jane's hand. "He's coming. In about an hour."

"Catch me up on your kids and your folks."

Patrice showed phone photos to go with the school reports and her mama's cooking, which was an art in itself. "You must try her jjigae. I'll have her make a batch for you when you're released. You like tofu? Veggies?"

"Yes," Jane said, although she'd tried tofu maybe twice in her life.

"Okay. Consider it done." She then went on to discuss her dad's antics with the football team Patrice's son played on.

"So any more talk about a long vacation in South Korea?"

"Nope. Not a word. They would not leave their grandchildren for the world."

"Yeah, my parents are like that too."

Jesse came in a while later. Jane kissed him and reminded Patrice that she needed to get her out of the hospital asap. Patrice promised to take care of it.

"I miss my dog," Jane told Jesse.

"You're feeling more like yourself?"

"Most of the time."

"We've got the place locked down like a fortress."

"But what if Hammer Man and his accomplice are *inside* the fortress?" Jane said.

"They are. But they are not in your building. We have uniforms on every floor every minute of every hour."

"See! I'll be safe."

Jesse didn't answer. He looked deeply into her eyes. Which was unlike him. What was he not telling her?

Chapter Thirty-One

A week later, when Jane's head felt clear as polished crystal, Patrice picked her up from the hospital and escorted her to her parent's home.

"Here's the plan," Patrice said. "We know 99 percent who the murderer is. The accomplice, if there is one, is not so obvious. We have items being tested, including DNA. We think it's a pair working together. We believe they thought the fake/original Frida was real. We surmise they needed the money. We are quite sure they live in Winding Bayou. That's why you are 'staying with your parents.' "

"I'm not staying with my parents?"

"No, ma'am. The murderous partners would expect that seeing as how it's common knowledge how close you are to your folks."

"Are my folks safe?"

"They are on Marco Island visiting friends."

"Snowbirds," Jane said. "I forget their name, but they're from my folks' hometown. Taylor, Michigan. I remember that." Jane squiggled around in her seat. "I feel like I just got out of jail!"

Patrice laughed. "Hospitals can be like that."

"So where am I going? Can I open the window?" Jane asked.

"Sure," Patrice said.

Jane pressed a button and let the breeze blow her

hair around. Silver strands in the wind. She pushed her face toward the sky. "The sun feels magnificent. It sure seems like we're heading to my parents' house."

"Seems being the key word."

"Where's Jesse?"

"He's following the man who is following us."

"Who is it!"

"A flunky, not the suspected killer. Whom we do not have solid evidence against yet anyway. They want to know where you go."

Jane checked her side window. Jesse so close! But if he was the car behind the car behind them, he was not in his own vehicle. "Why's Jesse driving a clunker?"

"You'll see. Hang on." Patrice floored it.

Jane twisted just in time to see Jesse change lanes and speed up. Then he was behind her. Then another car came out of a side street and wedged the flunky off the side of the road. Both Patrice and Jesse turned off onto the airport road. The flunky was out of his car taking photos.

Jesse switched from the beater to a white SUV at the airport. Jane traded cars, and Jesse hugged her while on duty. Not a normal Jesse move. Patrice pulled two suitcases from her trunk. Jane recognized them. Hers. Jesse took them and stowed them in the SUV. Patrice blew Jane a kiss. "Have fun, you two."

****

"I'm happy to see you and all, but where are we going?" Jane asked.

"Undercover."

"Cool," Jane said. She noticed Jesse had grown out his hair. It looked good on him. He had sun streaks too.

"You okay with getting some pink highlights or

181

lowlights or whatever they call them?"

"Where the heck are we going?"

"Panama City. Just for a few days."

"I'm not complaining."

Panama City was full of students on winter break. Or was it spring? "What month is it?" Jane asked Jesse. "What day?"

"February 9, 2020. It's a Tuesday, and I'm so glad you're okay."

They'd stopped, and Jane's hair had very nice pink extensions attached. She kind of liked them. They sat on the beach in their boomer swimsuits, Jane had a leopard print two-piece with boy-short bottoms and a modest neckline. She didn't have wrinkled cleavage yet, but this could be the day. Jesse wore new board shorts. Jane had a mocktail, and Jesse held an alcohol-free beer. The hotel had set out chaises, an umbrella, and a table for their drinks. Back in their suite, Jesse had presented Jane with a beach towel that said *Her Ladyship* while his said *His Lordship*. Not that they'd fool anyone, in fact they were invisible, even with Jane's blingy sandals and toe ring. Jesse's washboard abs were cut. No old guy gut for him. They made a perfect invisible middle-aged couple. Middle-aged if they lived to be 110.

The sun felt lovely. The hotel had a semiprivate patch of beach, nobody was anywhere around them, because the tiki bar cocktails were pricey beyond belief, and the chaises were only for guests. Still, lots of kids were playing volleyball or frisbee or splashing and laughing and drinking at the shore. Sometimes Jane got a whiff of marijuana.

Jane was not a prude, but she mentioned it to Jesse. Not like he was going to bust out his detective badge and arrest a bunch of college kids.

"Look on the bright side, Shug. You went to college, right?"

"Yeah, yeah. I also had kids who went to college. But Danny smoked pot in high school. As did I. Marisol, well, no, I think she's allergic."

"That's what she wants you to think."

For some reason, this cracked Jane up. She laughed so hard she fell off her chaise. Two college boys came over and asked Jesse if he needed help lifting her.

Jane stood on her own and brushed sand off her legs. "So, it takes three men to lift me, huh?"

The kids walked away laughing.

"They're just high," Jesse said. Typical police banter.

"You went to college, too, right?"

"Police college is different. We don't break laws in cop college."

"I can't keep straight which states are legal. Jesse. Will you tell me who is after me? You say you're 99 percent sure he's the killer. What's your proof? Why can't you tell me?"

"I can tell you. That's why we're here, so you don't go tearing up to the penthouse and confronting him."

"Ray?"

"Yes, Ray. We found a copy of Frida's diary during our second search in the same trunk where the angel wings were stored. A few feathers were still in the trunk. And we have Ray's fingerprint on the frame of the reproduction of Frida."

"It sure looks like he's guilty."

"We're eliminating other prints on the picture frame; we're looking for Ray's prints on the book, and a

few other fancy things with the feathers."

"The husband always does it! I knew it!"

"Well, we don't know it. Not for certain. We have been hunting down a dozen false leads on an accomplice. Biffy is proving interesting. Grant, too. It just takes time, Shug."

"I know, and being on vacation is fun. But I'm burned enough for today. Let's get cleaned up and go for a walk. That's safe, right?"

Jesse hesitated, then said maybe it would be okay.

"I got my big strong cop man to protect me. And I don't know why, but when I'm on vacation, even a fake two-day vacation, I feel the urge to shop."

"Me, too," Jesse said in the most deadpan voice. She almost fell off her chaise again from laughing.

Chapter Thirty-Two

Patrice answered a call from Kim.

"I'm worried about Jane."

"She's safe. She's with Jesse."

"Well, do you want to go have some dinner? What time do you get off shift?"

"I'll do dinner."

"Okay, great."

"In about a half hour. Let's go to that bar by the swing dance club in Largo," Patrice said.

"Someone is getting lonely," Kim said.

It was true. Patrice was lonely. And she'd discovered a love of swing dancing. Being held with no strings attached was awesome.

"That bar only has olives and limes in the food category," Kim said. "But we can go to the swing dance club tomorrow night."

"I'm not sure I can go out two nights in a row."

"I've met your mom. You can go."

"Well…"

"Let's go to Martini Joe's. It's halfway between us," Kim said. Patrice lived in Madeira Beach, and Kim lived at the northeast corner of St. Pete. Martini Joe's was in Seminole, the town between their two towns.

They ordered martinis and steaks. After, they had coffee on the patio so their single martini each had a chance to wear off. Patrice could tell Kim hoped she'd spill the tea on Jesse and Jane. Instead she told Kim about the detective sexually harassing her. He was getting less subtle by the day.

"I don't know what to do. I need this job. Cops are an old boys' club."

"Does Jesse know?" Kim said, once she was able to speak.

"No."

Kim was from another age. She was a boomer, like almost everyone in Winding Bayou, and Patrice was Gen X. Wasn't sexual abuse a huge boomer thing? Yes, but the women (and boys and girls) never told. Until they did. And by then it was too late. Too easy for the slimy men to slither away or say it was mutual or the memory could not be relied on. Instead of "me too" it was "not me."

After Kim got over her shock, she got mad. "I'm going in there and telling him I'm your mother, and he needs to stop hitting on you."

"That's sweet, but the chief knows my mom."

"Well. We'll think of something."

They were silent for a few minutes, sipping coffee, sobering up.

"I've got it," Kim said. "*You* solve the crime while Jesse is gone! Then, you out the dick who is creeping on you."

"It's a good plan, but we think we know who the killer is. We're just waiting on evidence."

"Like what? The hammer? And who is Hammer Man? You need to tell me!"

"We have the hammer. It was wiped clean of prints and left in the scrub at the fence line."

"Oh. Who is it? You can count on my discretion. I

will trap them into confessing. Or something."

"That's not a bad idea," Patrice said. Kim's jaw dropped. "But I really can't say. Except everyone is safe. He is under constant surveillance."

"Then let me guess."

Kim guessed and guessed, but she never got it right. Patrice didn't know if she was happy or sad about that. She wasn't happy, ever, these days except brief moments when her children hugged her or her mom made her favorite sugar rice or her dad smiled at her and called her "my girl." Never at work. She was okay as long as she was out on a case but not at the station.

"Are you crying?"

Patrice put her hand to her cheek. "I didn't know." She wiped the tears away.

"It's okay. Let's not talk about it. But you do need to talk about it."

"Yeah, I think I really do."

They walked into the parking lot and got in Kim's car, driving while Kim called Jane's mom. They reached Kim's as Jane's mom answered the phone. Kim opened the door and waved Patrice inside.

"Hi, Mrs. Chasen, this is Kim, Jane's friend. I have Patrice, Jesse's partner, here on speaker."

"Is Jane okay?" Patrice worried Jane's mom would cry too.

"Yes. Absolutely," Kim said. She figured, the less said the better.

"Great. Still, a mother never stops worrying." Mrs. Chasen drew a deep breath. "How can I help you, Patrice?"

Patrice sat at Kim's kitchen table, stunned silent.

"Patrice would you like to have a friendly talk?"

"Okay," Patrice said.

"We need neutral ground," Mrs. Chasen said.

"You can come over here. I'll go visit my friend Hazel," Kim said.

"Or we could go up to Jane's right now. I have a house key," Mrs. Chasen said. "I'm sure she wouldn't mind. How does that sound, Patrice?"

****

Mrs. Chasen made tea in the kitchen while Patrice sat in Jane's sunroom. Patrice missed Jane. She missed her partner. She felt frozen. She felt ashamed. Had being divorced somehow led to this thing with Tesper? All the words and thoughts were mixed and tripping over each other so that she couldn't even think about saying anything straight.

"Thanks," Patrice said, taking the cup of tea Jane's mom handed her.

After sipping tea in silence, Mrs. Chasen set down her cup. "This is just a talk between friends," she said. "I don't have a license anymore, but I can advise you and be an advocate if you'd like me to be with you when you take first steps. Sexual harassment is a big problem. It's so good you reached out before things turned even more intimate, which is actually intimidation. Just remember, it's not your fault. If it's happening to you, it's happening to other women in your department."

Patrice nodded. "I'm the only female detective. I don't want my parents to know. I don't want my kids to know, or my ex-husband."

"Do you want to keep your job?"

Sobs burst from deep in her diaphragm. She felt sick. She cried so hard she could not stop. Mrs. Chasen sat with her, witnessing her pain. Patrice didn't feel embarrassed or ashamed. That was the first clear thought that came out of her tangled mind. It wasn't her fault. Of course it wasn't. She'd wasted a lot of time wondering what she could have done different. How she'd brought this on. But she'd done nothing. It was all him. Tesper.

She accepted a tissue from Mrs. Chasen and blew her nose hard. She tucked the sopping tissue in her empty teacup. When had she drunk the tea? If thoughts were wheels, hers were slowing down, stopping. She'd cried it all out.

"I want to keep my job, but I don't want to work with Tesper. I want him to be fired. But I don't want publicity. I want to make him quit and go far away."

"Okay," Mrs. Chasen said. "I can help you with a few of those things. Keep your job. Keep what Tesper did internal and private. He'll want that too. What happens after that is up to the department."

"Where do we start?" Patrice's heart cracked open with hope.

"There are two ways to handle this. One is to report directly to HR. The second and most-used option is the one you chose: talking things over with family or trusted friends first, then when your head is clear, report every incident of harassment to HR."

"What are they going to ask me?"

"When did it start? How many times did it happen? Is it ongoing? What was your response? Specifics, like did he touch your breasts or butt or rub his penis against you? Did he say he wanted to have sex with you? That could be using words from 'rape' to 'fuck' to 'get with you.' Did things start small and escalate? Exactly how? Was the situation quid pro quo—that is did he offer you something in return for sex? Or was it more of what we call a toxic work environment? Dirty jokes? Gestures? You might want to write things down and refer to them when you have your interview with HR."

It was almost too much to take in. That was why she'd waited so long. That was why she recorded the conversation on her phone now. And later, she'd write it all down for the chief, from day one when Officer Tesper gave her a hug of congratulations for her promotion. He'd let his hand fall down her back and lightly skim her butt. He whispered, "You're a big girl now. But the higher you climb, the faster you fall. These guys are animals, as you know. They can't wait to take you down. I can help you stay on top." He squeezed her butt and smiled like an old friend. It was true he wanted detective. It was true he'd been on the force longer than she had. His opening move had not been subtle. Quid pro quo, as Mrs. Chasen said.

"But it's not quid pro quo," Patrice said. "He helped me not one bit. He will help me not one bit. I have a good partner, the best. I don't need anything from him. Did you know Jesse has daughters? Both of them single and beautiful. Tesper could be harassing them. And that will be on me if I don't tell Jesse what's going on. But I don't want to put him in the middle of my problem. It's not fair. He's not here, anyway. Oh, it's happening again." Patrice held her head in her hands and rubbed her temples in circles.

"Breathe," Mrs. Chasen said, breathing steadily loud enough for Patrice to follow her lead.

After a minute, Patrice's audible breathing steadied. "I never knew breathing could be so loud," she remarked. "And, thanks, I know this will be hard, and I appreciate your help. Please don't tell Jane."

"Honey, of course not. This evening never leaves the vault."

After Jane's mom left, Patrice felt frozen to the sofa.

Kim walked in. "You okay, kiddo?"

Patrice shrugged. "She's amazing, but no way do I like any of this."

"Well, of course you don't!"

"Please don't tell Jane," Patrice said.

They heard the door open, and the wheeled suitcases coming down the hall.

"Don't tell Jane what?" Jane said.

Chapter Thirty-Three

Jane was cranky. She'd envisioned coming home from Panama City and flopping on the sofa while a frozen pizza baked in the oven. Instead here were Kim and Patrice. Her good friends. Patrice was in immediate conference mode with Jesse. Had there been a break in the case? Jane gave Kim a quick hug. "I have got to visit the ladies room. *Now*."

"You can try, but there ain't no ladies here. It's the women's room. Or if you're southern for real, a powder room."

Jane waved and scooted down the hall to her bedroom and private bath.

Once she was alone behind closed doors, she thought about Jesse's offer. Stay here or stay with him. She'd not yet been to Jesse's house. He lived outside town in one of those rare coastal areas that hadn't been condo-developed and populated overnight by Michiganders like her. Unincorporated Crooked Nook. You could not get mail there; well, you could, but it would be marked St. Petersburg. Crooked Nook had no post office. It had a little grocery store, Jesse said, but no downtown. It had never been a town. Thus it was a good hideout.

A knock on her door made her drop the facecloth with which she'd been scrubbing off her makeup. She hated her startle reflex, which had only gotten worse with age. "Coming," she said, plucking the cloth off the floor and tossing it in the laundry basket in the corner.

"Hi, Patrice. I was surprised to see you here."

Patrice looked devastated.

"Is this about that officer who's been harassing you?"

"Yes. I told Kim, and she had me talk to your mom. And just now she forced me to tell Jesse. Well, not forced, but she made me see it made sense. Your mom just left; she agreed Jesse and the chief need to be told. Tesper used to be Jesse's partner, and I kind of stole Jesse from him, in a way. And this is payback. Or anyway, that's your mother's theory. Jesse is not taking it well."

"I'm coming. Let's go out there and discuss what's to be done."

"I'm sorry," Patrice said. "You look tired."

"It's okay. You are priority one right now."

Jesse looked angry as a snapping gator. Kim was gone. Jane was glad Belle was still with her parents. Belle sensed tension, and it made her little body shake like she was revving up for a stakeout.

"I'm sorry, Jesse," Patrice said.

"Don't be. Tesper's always been an asshole. This is it. I've had it with him."

"Patrice has to go to HR," Jane said.

"Tomorrow," Jesse said.

"It's his word against mine."

"I was his partner for nine years. I saw plenty. It's his word against *ours*."

Patrice straightened her back. Jane was happy to see her looking her brave self again instead of beaten down.

"Jesse. Let me pack a bag, and I'll come with you."

"You're going to Crooked Nook?" Patrice said.

"I am."

"But nobody's been there. Ever."

"Don't I know it," Jane said, who had to be the target of an almost serial killer to get an invitation. "And Belle is coming."

"How is that going to work? What's the plan for getting rid of the tail—"

While Patrice and Jesse talked strategy, Jane went to pack a bag. She loaded her Kindle with books as she'd forgotten to ask Jesse if he had internet. Sure he did. He was a cop. Still, she bought the fourteen-book series of a first novel she'd seen on television. One could only read Jane Austen so many times. Once a year, to be precise. This Regency series would bridge a bit of the gap. She could not take murder mysteries when she was living one. Then she called her mom to say someone would be picking up Belle today.

"You?"

"I'm not sure. Jesse and Patrice are working it out. They're stashing Belle and me out on Crooked Nook."

"You don't say! Fort Knox, Florida, then."

"Yeah. I'll be safe."

"You better be, or your father will have something to say to Jesse."

"I love you, too, Mom."

"How's...how's Patrice?"

"She talked to you. Never mind, it's a good thing. She's going to report Tesper tomorrow."

"Good for her. Will you call me? Every day?"

"I'll try. I don't know the plan yet."

"It will all work out. I love you."

After the call to her mom, Jane's hands trembled as

she folded clean clothes into her large wheelie. Then she refilled her weekender with more skin products, cosmetics, Kindle, and iPad. She didn't have a suitcase for Belle; it was at her mom's with Belle's favorite things. She brightened at the idea of having Belle to protect her. A trained police dog. They could walk on the beach, at least Jane hoped they could. She finished her packing quickly, her anxiety turning into adrenaline.

She found a little space in her smaller suitcase for the pills her doc had given her the last time this sort of thing had happened. Not that long ago. Was this what dating a cop was like? Jesse had assured her that it was not normal in St. Pete for two murderers to strike within six weeks of each other. "Unheard of," he'd said.

"You ready, Shug?"

"I am."

Jane wheeled both suitcases out to the hallway.

"Where's Patrice?"

"Creating a diversion so we can get out of here. Now."

Jane locked the door behind her.

She saw Dennis and Rusty down two doors at her place. Both cats were on their leashes. Dennis held one leash.

"Going away again?" Rusty yelled in a jolly voice.

"Where to this time?" Dennis called.

Jane waved and smiled and nodded but didn't say anything. Jesse didn't bother to acknowledge them. It was kind of cute how he was jealous of Dennis. They stopped at Barb and George's place, where Jesse had a quiet conference with Barb. "A courtesy," he said once they were on the road.

George's hair was a huge mess and too long, but not

artful in any way. He was deep into his screenplay and detailed the problems he was having with the script to Jane. "Watch out for your wife," Jane said.

"Oh, she's watching out for me. There's only one tough guy in this condo, and it's her…that's a great line. I gotta get back to work. Be safe."

In the car again, Jesse was explaining that he wanted to keep pregnant Barb in the loop "as an overabundance of caution."

"What you mean is they really want me. And only me."

"Now, Jane. I've got you. No worries, right? Caution, but you're safe at Crooked Nook."

"I've been reading about serial killers. He left that picture of me that he stole from my photo album—you've seen all my photo albums—but he found that one picture and he left it by my head as if to say 'I'll be back.' He's some kind of whacko and why does he hate me? I'm nice to everyone!"

"You are, Shug. Did you bring those meds?"

"Are you saying I need meds?"

"No, not at all. Just your nerves are a bit on edge," Jesse said.

"Yeah, I got 'em. But it's being here in this condo. How did Ray get in here and how did he find that photo?"

"Another reason we don't want you staying here. There must be a duplicate key floating around," Jesse said.

"Kim has my dupe, and she would not let it out of her sight."

"For now, you can't be here."

"I could get my lock changed, but I agree. I don't want to be here. I'm still nervous," Jane said.

"Belle will help," Jesse consoled.

"That dog is the best medicine. And our little getaway together, of course," Jane said.

"I'm staying with you tonight on Crooked Nook, but I have to go back to the case tomorrow. And stand with Patrice."

"Because protecting me is work."

"Yes, but it's work I enjoy." Jesse smiled widely, refreshed by their getaway.

So was she. Now she was going to Crooked Nook. But first, Belle. They pulled into the groomers, where Belle had been shampooed and had her teeth brushed and her nails clipped. Jesse said it was a gift from her mom, but Jane knew it was a precaution. If the killer thought she was with her parents…well, they had a 24-hour guard. But still. Jane worried.

Belle yipped with joy as she saw her two favorite people, but she didn't jump or lick Jane's face because she'd been trained in no-nonsense behavior. Still her little butt wiggled, and her tail wagged. Jane picked up her pooch and hugged her, which was permission to let ecstasy loose. She licked Jane's jaw and snuggled into her neck, where she fell asleep. Going to the dog salon wore Belle out.

Jesse gave them the side eye. They were driving, and Belle should be in her crate in the back seat. He didn't say anything, just sighed.

Chapter Thirty-Four

Crooked Nook had seemed anything but crooked until suddenly a white beach house appeared at the end of a long, long straight road, on a large piece of land curled like a shrimp tail. Jesse pulled his car into the first-floor garage.

"Welcome to my humble abode," he said.

"I was laughing because 'crooked' didn't match the description of the landscape until the very last minute."

"I know that, Shug. It's the joke of the town."

"Town? What town? I didn't see any town."

Jesse laughed too. "And that's the way we like it."

"No wonder you said I wouldn't need my car. There's nowhere to go."

Belle, still in Jane's arms, barked and sniffed the salty Gulf air. She knew walks came with that scent.

"Okay, girl. Hang on a minute." Jane turned to Jesse. "I should let her do her business."

"Yes. Let me show you."

They were so close to the water they heard the waves before they saw them.

Belle tugged Jane to a little garden area, beach roses growing on a trellis. She relieved herself with a dainty curtsy.

"Good girl." Jesse had a treat ready. Belle's tail swished as she carefully took the treat.

"I'll get the luggage. Door's open. Go on in and

check it out. Not much to see but the water, and then there's the sunset."

"How'd you unlock the door?" Jane hoped this wasn't the kind of community where nobody locked their doors. She did have a sort of serial killer after her, although Jesse had assured her he was in Winding Bayou and they'd know the minute he left the property. She felt safe-ish as she grabbed Belle's tote and headed to the stairs on the side of the house, Belle by her side.

"You been here, haven't you? I know, I know. Your first home away from that nasty academy training school."

She stopped on the first step and asked Jesse, "How long did Belle stay with you before you brought her to me?"

"About two hours. I had to do some paperwork, then we picked up the special vegan dog food."

"That is just amazing. She remembers this place."

"Beagles are very smart dogs."

"Especially Belle."

At the top of the stairs, Jane turned a corner and there was the Gulf of Mexico, spangled with sun, a priceless jewel. The slider door behind her forgotten, she set down Belle's tote and leaned on the white balcony rail. Belle whined to be let off her leash, so Jane reached down and released her. The balcony was only on the front of the house, so Belle couldn't take off out of sight, not that she would.

Jesse came out the slider door. "Haven't made it in yet?"

"How'd you get done unloading so fast?" Jane asked.

"There's an elevator in the garage, but I thought

you'd like this way."

"It's gorgeous, Jesse." Jane tucked a curl behind her ear and checked her pedicure. Jane had never had a pedicure before she moved to Florida, but with a shoe wardrobe consisting of mostly sandals, pedicures were an essential part of grooming. As important as a haircut. And the beachy colors on her toes never failed to cheer her up.

"I'll put Belle's bed in the front room. Not that she'll sleep for a while."

"I should give her a drink of water," Jane said.

"And we can have a glass of wine out here if you like." He gestured to the wide slatted-wood beach chairs, painted yellow and graced with fat pillows, also yellow, printed with white anchors.

Jane plopped into one of them. "You? Wine?"

"Okay, okay. So wine makes my teeth hurt. I'll have a beer. Just one."

"As opposed to the 'just one more' you had in Panama City?"

"I want to be in top shape when Patrice and I confront Tesper tomorrow morning."

"Guess I should check out your bachelor pad."

"I've never brought a woman here, Shug."

"Well, can't say that anymore. You got a drawer or two for me?"

Jesse put his arm around her and squeezed. "The tour awaits."

The beach house only had two rooms, but they were large. Living room and kitchen combined, then bedroom with bath. The rooms were painted oyster shell white, and the furniture was simple and sparse.

"Sofa, table, chair, bed. Stools on the peninsula.

Built-in drawers in the closet. You're a minimalist." Everything was in neutral colors, even the lamps. Nothing on the walls except two framed photos of his teenaged daughters, Gulf in the background. One with both of them kissing him, one to each cheek. Very sweet.

Jesse shrugged. "Easier to clean."

Belle lapped at her water in the kitchen. Jesse poured Jane a glass of Chardonnay in a cut-crystal wine glass.

"Wow. That's my favorite label. And what a glass."

"Family heirloom. The glass, not the wine." He grabbed a beer from the fridge, and they went out to the balcony. Jesse put his beer on the rail and opened the table between the beach chairs. Jane sat. This time she noticed the cushions were the most comfortable she'd ever melted into. Her bones whispered thank you.

As the sun set, the sparkles skimming the water turned coral. Belle made up for missing her beach walk by patrolling the balcony, barking at sea birds, and playing tug of war with Jesse and her beloved knotted rope. Jane sighed, relaxed as she could be with someone determined to make her his next victim.

"It's been a long time since lunch, Shug. You hungry?"

Belle barked yes.

"I could eat," Jane said.

"Groceries were delivered today. Let's see what they brought."

"Jesse, does the grocery store fly in food with a helicopter? And do they have a key?"

"No to both. My phone unlocks the door, and I see them on camera the entire time they're in the house."

"You got some high-tech lifestyle. James Bond

2020. How long does it take to get here from downtown?"

"Half an hour."

"Not too terrible."

Jesse pulled cheese, mustard, salami, and ham from the fridge. "I thought we'd have sandwiches. Anything else on yours?"

He held the door open while Jane grabbed avocado, lettuce, and tomato. She turned to the countertop and saw Belle at her feet, waiting with urgent patience by her food bowl. "That's right, baby. You're hungry, too."

After dinner they tried to watch television, but it had been a long day. Belle went down first. Jesse next. Jane couldn't settle. She tried not to dwell on who had a duplicate of her key. And how. Her head hurt so she took a pain pill, but it did not help her solve this puzzle.

Chapter Thirty-Five

When she woke, Jane was surprised she'd slept. She'd spent half the night worrying about who had a duplicate of her key and how things would go with Patrice, too. Jesse's clock read 6:10. She heard his shower. Smelled the coffee. Reached down to scratch Belle's head. Belle moaned. Not knowing Jesse's policy about dogs in bed, Jane got up instead of inviting Belle for a cuddle as was their custom at home.

Home. She'd loved Winding Bayou, but the allure had disappeared now George and Barb were leaving. And someone else had been in her house, intending to do her harm and scare the crap out of her while they were at it. Sure she had nice neighbors and there was always going to be Kim…

"Good, you found the coffee," Jesse said. He kissed her quick. Jane refused entry to the anxiety and sadness knocking. People had jobs, important jobs. Life was not a perpetual vacation, even when you were retired. The jitters started even before she finished her first cup of coffee. Jesse had prepped a to-go cup, so he took a sip of hers.

"Couple of things we didn't quite get to last night," he said.

Jane faked ease. She smiled at Belle, then lifted her face and kept that smile in place as she met Jesse's eyes. He opened a cupboard and showed her the toaster.

"Walnut cranberry bread in the fridge. Please make yourself at home."

"Okay," Jane said.

"Are you nervous? You look a little scared."

"Well, I am, for Patrice. I haven't got to worrying about myself yet."

"Then let me set your mind to rest. No more James Bond comments, though."

"Promise."

He turned a switch next to the pantry, and the doors slid silently open. This was not a pantry; it was the elevator she'd forgotten all about. "Okay, come on down." They stepped in the elevator, Belle following.

"She's probably got business by the rosebushes."

"Yes."

After they walked over to the little garden and Belle did her tinkle curtsy, Jesse led Jane back into the garage. "The remote on this here thing is bullet-proof. Nobody can get in but me, or whoever holds the remote." He handed Jane a remote with a key on it. "Therefore, I don't lock the elevator. The remote activates it." He did a demo. Just a push of the remote. A red light blinked on and held steady next to E. "This is the door, aptly labeled D."

"And I bet the A is for auto."

"Bingo!"

"Did this cost a million dollars?"

Jesse laughed. "You haven't met my brother yet. He's brilliant at tech. Lives in San Francisco. He set this all up for me. Birthday present." Jane realized she didn't know Jesse's birthday. Or how she could ever top this gift.

"There's one more thing that makes this a really safe

fortress."

"Besides the fact that you never have visitors?"

"The girls come when they can. The sofa folds out into a bed. But they're only here when I'm home. And you're here now. I'll invite the girls to meet you. My twins. They live with my ex-wife, but they like camping on my sofa. In fact, my brothers promised to build them a place on one of the other lots so they don't have to sleep in my living room. My younger brother is a senior at Cal Tech. He started college later in life after a career as a lifeguard. My older has been in Silicon Valley forever. But they'll visit soon. They promised."

"Then there's Belle."

Jesse grinned. "You will love this."

"Let's see!" Jane's anxiety had floated away somewhere around the time he'd given her a key to his house.

"So if you can't get in through the garage or the elevator, which nobody can except me and you, unless I personally allow them entry, that leaves the stairs." Jesse walked over to the open garage door and turned the corner to the stairs. "Come here where I'm standing."

Jane did.

"Hold Belle."

Jane gathered the pup into her arms. Belle licked her chin.

Jesse went back to the middle of the garage and clicked S. The stairway moved on tracks into the garage from the side of the house. Jane's head swiveled. The stairs were in the garage. Several locking devices bolted with a slight noise into place. Jane dipped her head and popped into the garage where Belle scrambled to get onto her own four feet.

"Now you tell me how anybody gets in this house except me and you."

"Don't you mean Bat Cave 2020?" Jane felt awe. She was thrilled, maybe dreaming.

Jesse laughed. She loved how she could make him laugh.

"So, no windows in the garage."

"Nada."

"What's the key for?"

"Oh. That's my work car key. You've got my duplicate. In case I should misplace the original. I should probably take that key off, but I'm running late. Buzz me upstairs."

"What?"

"We're doing a run-through."

"Oh. Yeah." She pressed E. The elevator opened. "Come, Belle!" Jane said.

Jesse came too. If only it were that easy on a normal day to get him to obey.

In the elevator, she pressed the up arrow and the doors swung open with a whisper. Belle barked and ran into the house.

"Let's go on the balcony. By the way, if someone brings a ladder and tries to breach the balcony, push the ladder over."

"Got it." Jane thought he was kidding. Hoped.

Once in a position to see where the stairway started, Jane pressed S. The stairs creaked out into the open.

"Gotta oil those gears," Jesse said.

"Regular home maintenance."

"Exactly. Now I really have to go. But I'm quite confident you'll be safe."

"I'll be certain if he shows up with a ladder to push

him to his possible death."

"All right then, Shug, I'm glad."

"You better go. Patrice needs your support. I won't ask when you'll be home, but I'll have dinner made."

"I'll call on the way."

"Thanks."

And he was gone. As soon as the garage was locked up, Jane enclosed the stairway. Shoot, she should have taken Belle out for a curtsy first.

Chapter Thirty-Six

Patrice and Jesse sat in front of the chief's desk. The chief was there, obviously pissed. Someone from HR sat in a corner on the sofa against the wall. Tesper's chair was empty. The chief had called the meeting, and Tesper didn't make it on time. Patrice could not believe he'd be one minute late, not fifteen. How had Jesse partnered with him for all those years? It did explain why he never got the expected promotion.

"Let's get this started," said the HR person. "Give me the background, Detective. When did these incidents start?"

"When I got the promotion to detective after the November 2019 murder solve."

"Tesper had been my partner for years," Jesse said, "and he was taking yet more time off, vacation this time, not medical. I saw how hard Patrice worked, knew she wanted detective, and asked you to advance her temporarily to Tesper's position when the homicide came out of nowhere. Tesper was not pleased when he got back."

Patrice knew what was coming next and tried to distract herself. But then there it was.

"And can you take me through the first incident, exactly as it happened?"

Tesper knocked and opened the door. "Sorry I'm late." He looked around, the bastard, like he was surprised to see the gathering. "Is this an intervention? Because I don't drink," Tesper said.

Fucker. Patrice was getting angry. Not scared. Good. It felt good to be angry. She took everyone, including Tesper, through his many forms of harassment since she'd made detective. She remembered each and every one. Each day, every form the fondling took, which dirty words he spoke.

Nobody said a word. She realized she was the only woman in the room. They couldn't have gotten a woman from HR? She'd finished what she had to say, and she didn't say anything else. Not even "I'm done," although she was.

"And how did this affect your work?"

"I'm dealing with a divorce, my parents have moved in, and I have a new job I love. None of it affects my work."

"Except for the whining and hallucinations," Tesper said, earning him a one-word reprimand from the chief.

"Enough!"

"Detective Singer, will you speak to your partner's ability to do her job?"

Patrice had had her say. She and Jesse were a great team. Nothing worried her except they were wasting time when they could be catching the murderer.

"She's the best partner I've ever had. Tesper was useless. Lazy. Derogatory toward women in general, whether witnesses or suspects. Not to their faces but later in the vehicle. He'd make jokes about their bodies. He said inappropriate things to me about Detective Riley."

This was news to Patrice.

"Such as?"

Jesse had never told her a word about Tesper talking

bad about her. He wouldn't. He'd try to shelter her feelings. That was Jesse. She was so glad he was here.

"He asked if she blew me just the once to get the promotion or if it was a regular thing," Jesse said. "One example." Jesse turned to face her. "Sorry, Patrice. I put him in his place."

"Jesse has a girlfriend, who is my friend, you asshole," Patrice said. She had never cussed in the chief's presence before, and today she'd fired off several swears in a row. Nobody said anything about it.

"Officer Tesper, is it accurate to say you feel you deserved the promotion?"

"Yes. And she's lying. So is he. Any witnesses, Patti?"

"I'll ask the questions," the HR guy said.

Men and their possessiveness when it came to their duties, Patrice thought.

"There are a few officers who saw some of what he did." She named names. "Not sure they'll stand up for me."

"They'll stand up for you," Jesse said.

How stupid men were about relationships in general. Not Jesse. Not the chief. But most of them. Sure, she was a nice person. She was nice to everyone. And she'd heard many times that guys from high school thought she had a crush on them, or wanted them, and it was never true. She was just being herself. They said she was flirting. By the time she'd hired into the PD, she knew not to smile. Not to be nice. Not to bring a cupcake or a card for a birthday. The only thing she'd ever done for another cop was buy a supply of pencils for Jesse, because he never had one.

Chapter Thirty-Seven

Jane, alone in the extreme security of Jesse's house, called Kim.

"What's new in the Bayou?" Jane asked.

"Well. Hazel and Ethan are planning a cruise as soon as this murder investigation is over."

"They deserve it." Jane still thought they were an odd couple, but they meant no harm. That counted for a lot.

"Lemme see. What else is new?" Kim said. "Ray and Biffy have crowned themselves King and Queen of the Bayou. Dennis and Rusty walk the cats daily. Biffy denied Abigail had an affair with Ray when Marva was still alive...what else? Grant has put a sign on the pool that renters cannot swim in it, or sun on the chaise lounges, only owners."

"That's against the law."

"I know! I called Barb. She said she'd get on it." Kim was a long-term renter. And an avid swimmer and sunbather.

"Are Barb and George doing okay?"

"Oh yeah. George says they have a 'working draft' of his script, whatever that means."

"Wedded bliss," Jane remarked. It felt good to catch up with her friend, even over the phone. "How about you? You okay?"

Kim sighed. "I'm mad at Grant for kicking me out

of my pool. I miss you. I'm a little scared. I wonder who the murderer is."

Jane wanted to tell her so bad. But she knew Kim was safe. "Jesse says the killer left that photo of me kidding around in the Frida mask next to my head when he knocked me out as a message." Jesse had told her no such thing, but when Patrice had let slip about the photo, Jane put two and two together. She knew it would calm Kim down to hear Jesse's opinion, even though it creeped her out that yet another murderer had been in her house. Her bedroom. Her drawers!

"What? Like he's going to cut your head off?"

Jane winced. Maybe she should not have called Kim, but it was nice to hear the neighborhood gossip. She was betting on Abigail and Ray having a fling sooner than later. Then Biffy would blow her top.

"I think maybe slit my throat. It's really difficult to decapitate someone."

"Yeah, the bones and whatnot," Kim said.

"Exactly."

"Ethan might know how to dissect a head from a torso. He seems to know a lot about science."

"Is it dissect or detach?"

"Well, dissect seems more medical-ish," Kim said.

"True."

"And what is the sense of knowing fancy words like dissect if you can't use them in conversation from time to time?"

"Also true," said Jane.

"How's Belle?"

"She's good. Napping." Jane knew when Belle woke up she was going to need to curtsy. She would have to activate the hidden staircase.

"Well, the cats miss her. That's what Dennis and Rusty say, anyway."

"They sure did fall in love fast."

"I think he was lonely. She had the cats, so she was fine on her own. But that Dennis. He seems the type who can't be without a little woman to fuss over him. Or maybe he's gonna make a sort of mini penthouse by knocking the wall out between their two condos."

Jane thought about it. Dennis was very friendly. Rusty not so much. She was shy, Jane had always thought. Dennis had brought her out of her shell. "Maybe," Jane said, feeling disloyal to Dennis but not wanting to argue with Kim.

A frenzied bark broke the second of silence.

"Belle is awake!" Kim said, laughing.

Belle never woke up barking. She didn't say anything to Kim about it. Why worry her? "I better go and tend to the princess," she said instead.

"Understood. Take care of yourself."

Jane always did, but sometimes things got out of hand. Like now. Belle barked and ran around in circles. If someone was outside, how could she take Belle to the rose garden? She texted Jesse just as she heard the stairway rumble out of hiding. She texted again. —*Is that you?*— Her heart beat like a wild bongo when he didn't respond.

"Need to let Belle out?" Jesse said, stepping from the too-silent elevator. "I figured she'd want to go down the stairs." Belle had been a bit awed by the elevator yesterday.

Belle was too well-trained to pee on the floor, but Jane translated her whimper as "yes, please."

"Yes, we were going down the stairs. I activated

them, but she was barking like a crazy girl, then I heard the elevator and texted you and you didn't answer and I…well, I freaked out a bit. Let's go, girl."

"Sorry, Shug. I didn't hear my phone. And I'm here now. And by the way, that's Belle's happy bark."

She nodded, embarrassed at being afraid, angry at Jesse for scaring her out of her wits, not texting, and making her feel like she needed a pill. Also she suspected he didn't want to take a chance Belle would curtsy in his elevator. She kissed him anyway since he was the only person who stood between her and possible beheading and led Belle down the stairs.

Chapter Thirty-Eight

The chief had dismissed Patrice and Jesse but kept Tesper back with the HR guy. Then Jesse said he "had a feeling" about Jane's safety and was going to run home and check on her.

Patrice loved Jane like a sister, but at this point she felt a little sting. True, she felt guilty about it, yet it was there. Partners stuck together. "Damn, girl, grow up," Patrice told herself. She tackled some filing Jesse had left for her. She read every file to keep herself sharp on the deeper points of the case.

"Detective Riley, in my office please."

The chief had come out to personally escort her. That made up a little bit for Jesse not being there to fend off smart remarks from uniforms who should know better.

"Jesse's on the job, as I'm sure you're aware, but you're needed for this last bit with HR. It may get rough in there," he said before opening his office door, "but I appreciate you keeping this an internal problem. Don't worry. I got your back. Tesper's a pain in my ass. If I could transfer him to Siberia, I would."

When they entered the room, Tesper sat there with a smirk on his face. Patrice's hand tingled to slap it off.

The chief lifted her complaint from his desk and read directly off it. "Toxic work environment, gender discrimination, sexual assault."

"Yep," Patrice said.

"Any chance you could label the assault harassment?" HR guy said.

"No, but I can add harassment to the assault," Patrice said.

"So, there was assault and harassment," said HR guy.

"Yes."

"And was the assault an isolated incident?

"No."

"We've gone over the incidents," the chief said. "There was more than one assault."

"Two. Correct?" HR guy looked at Patrice like she was the enemy, the betrayer of cops everywhere.

"Yes. Things were escalating. I worried rape would be next."

Tesper laughed. "You wish."

The chief frowned and wrote something on his pad of paper. "That was uncalled for, Tesper, and can be considered harassment in itself. Am I right?" The chief looked at HR guy, who nodded once, very slightly.

Tesper's face turned red. Patrice would never believe he was actually embarrassed by his actions. She read him as angry. The culture of many police departments overlooked excessive use of force, certain abuses of the integrity of the badge, down to foul language and berating women officers and worse. It was just the way it was. But when it happened to her, Patrice was still surprised. She loved her job and most cops were decent people.

"I'll accept him transferring to another state. Like Alaska," Patrice said, knowing that was not how law enforcement worked. Just thinking about her situation made her ready to bring a case against the department.

The chief lifted the sheet of paper he'd been scribbling on. "I can attest, just from what I've seen here today and by Detective Riley's written sworn oath and that of her partner, that Tesper's actions are unacceptable."

"Whaa..." Tesper started.

"Unprofessional," the chief added as if Tesper had not spoken. "You've blackened the reputation of this PD, also, and worst, what you've done is unlawful."

The HR man nodded from his corner on the couch.

"Okay, we have a bit more business here, but Detective Riley, you can get back to the job," the chief said. "I know you'll catch this guy."

Patrice left. She had no friends on the force except Jesse. She never had. That had always been okay by her. She had a home and family. She was busy, and her friendships with Kim and Jane made a refreshing change from the men in blue. Being the only woman officer, then the only female detective, she understood people were angry and jealous over her being favored, chosen to partner Jesse when Tesper took his many vacations and sick leaves.

She wished Jesse would get back. She wished Tesper would go to hell.

Chapter Thirty-Nine

"Why are you home so early?" Jane asked Jesse as they walked the beach with Belle. Amazing. Tourist season and the beach was empty.

"You're my job, Shug. Not just my sweetie."

She went on tiptoes to kiss him on the cheek. Belle walked on the beach side and barked politely at the water when it hit Jane's knees and almost bowled her over. Jesse put his arm around her to keep her from falling in the waves, which were deeper with a stronger undercurrent than they appeared.

"Why is nobody here? This is a lovely beach."

"Snowbirds don't come this far down. You can't see it from the shoreline because it's crooked inland a little bit. Also, no tiki bar or umbrellas for rent."

"Any hard evidence yet?"

"We've got all his tools being examined. Boy is he mad, called me the cop from hell." Jesse chuckled. "I'm sorry, Shug. It's not funny."

"We're still working on a warrant for the accomplice. Today we're on Grant. We need to go through his office, his laptop, all of it. Until we have that warrant, at least we can keep an eye on him."

His phone rang. "Patrice," he said, answering. "You don't say! Good job, partner. Yeah, I'll be in." He listened for a minute. "Okay. You come here. I'll text you directions."

He turned to Jane. "Patrice wants to know if you'd like a martini and a steak. She's buying."

Jane smiled. "Yes! Perfect. Except we have everything here."

Jesse had bent down and released Belle's leash. He dug a tennis ball out of his pocket and played catch with Belle on the sand.

"I have to run a lead down. I can do it online after dinner."

"Is the case breaking?"

"It's Patrice's complaint. I'll let her tell you all about it."

Jane feigned surprise.

"I know you two talk. Shug, this is personal. I think she's more comfortable talking to you about sexual harassment than to me."

"Yeah." Jane had forgotten Patrice's traumatic experiences for the brief time they were on the beach. "I'm going to shower."

"Me too," Jesse said. "No rest for the weary."

"Come on, Belle. Race you up the stairs."

Belle started racing and beat Jane easily.

After Belle shook herself off, the beach house floor was covered in sand. "Where's your vacuum? After I shower, I'll clean this up," Jane said.

"Hmm. The cleaning lady brings it."

Jane called Patrice to stop at the big box store and grab a vacuum cleaner.

Patrice grumbled at that. "Jane, I've got big news!"

"But it's right on the way!" Jane thought again about all Patrice had been through. "Never mind, dumb idea. And skip the steaks and martinis, we've got those too. Jesse's barbecuing."

Jane hung up. "You got a broom?" she asked Jesse.

"Yes, of course." Jesse pulled a broom from a closet and swept up the sand.

"Patrice said her information is vital."

Jesse made an O out of his mouth. "More vital than a vacuum cleaner?" He sent Jane a text with the cleaning lady's phone number. "She'll clean, do a grocery run if you need vodka or vegan dog food." He texted the cleaning lady about his guests, Jane and Belle.

"She doesn't have a key?" Jane worried.

"Nope. She texts me when she arrives. I open the garage and the elevator and turn on the cameras. Close them when she leaves."

That made Jane feel better.

"Shug, I hate to break it to you, but we're running late. We're gonna have to shower together."

"Not a problem, detective." She loved when he scrubbed her back.

****

Jane's hair was almost dry when Patrice got there. The martinis were dry, too, and garnished with Spanish Queen olives stuffed with blue cheese.

"Hold those in the fridge, Shug, and let Pat in."

Jane used the remote device like a pro, and Patrice swooshed up the elevator.

"Very nice," Patrice said.

Jane shut the garage door and hugged Patrice. "Sorry, the boss says we need to wait on the martinis until you tell us what's going on with Tesper." Jane opened the fridge to set the pitcher of martinis inside. Three filets sat glistening in the fridge, ready for the barbecue.

"Any news from the Bayou?" Jesse asked Patrice.

"All's quiet. Pool's being cleaned, so Grant's supervising that."

Jane said, "Jesse told me who you guys like for the murder."

Patrice nodded. "A woman should know the name of man who is aiming to slice her head off."

Jane shuddered and reached for her extra-roomy peach sweater, pulling it around herself.

"Okay, Patrice, take us through your day. Starting with Tesper after I left. What's been decided?" Jesse said.

"Well, he's guilty as hell. He even harassed me in front of the chief! We came to an internal agreement that starting tomorrow Tesper will have an indefinite leave of absence. Unpaid. Or he can take early retirement. No trial."

Jane knew Patrice would not like a trial either.

"It's actually great. He'll retire. The chief forced the issue, really," Patrice said. "So then I was filing like you told me, Jesse, and I decided to have one more look at all the paperwork. Just to see if we missed something."

"Good idea. And you found…," Jesse said.

"Well, just by chance I put this together. Abigail was on the original list with her phone number."

"Yeah. Abigail worked in the office for a time," Jane said.

"We didn't know that."

"I didn't know it was important." Jane wondered if Abigail could have duped her key when Bill, the office manager, was on vacation. She wanted to tell Patrice and Jesse, but she waited until Patrice could get her story out.

"She's friends with Grant," Patrice said. "There's more, Jesse, and you're not going to like it."

221

"Hit me."

"Your shopping-cleaning lady? She has the same details as Abigail. Phone. Address. License plate."

Jesse thought out loud. "Her name is Gail. I didn't interview her; she wasn't a suspect at first. Somebody else talked to her, and I read the report. I've never really seen her except on camera and her license photo. Online interview. I hired her to clean while I worked or spent time with Jane. I checked references; they all said she was a great cleaner and everyone knew her as Gail."

"Why bother to have a secret secure house and then let in a random Gail?" Patrice said.

"Does Gail stand for Abigail?" Jesse was defensive. "Her social security card is under Gail. So, Abigail must be...I don't know, an alternate name she uses and now we might know why. As for security here, give me some credit. She has been inside of course, but only through the garage and up the elevator while on camera. She's on camera in the house too."

"Where were the steps?"

"Outside. They're typically outside."

"Okay. How is she with cleaning?"

"Quick and efficient. Thirty minutes and out. Laundry day maybe ninety minutes."

Patrice had her recorder on. "How many times does she come a week?"

"Twice. Tuesday and Thursday. She does the laundry and scrubs the bathrooms on Tuesday. Thursday she brings groceries and cleans the kitchen."

"When does she vacuum?" Jane asked.

"Tuesday."

"What if..." Jane's brain gears seemed rusty. They slowly moved. "Could Abigail be the accomplice?" Jane mentioned about the keys. "I don't see a man breaking into my condo to sort through photos."

"Does not sound like a guy thing. We can veer off Grant. That's going nowhere. Onto Abigail. And there's still Biffy," Patrice said.

"Jesse! What if Abigail cased your house while we were in Panama City?" Jane moaned. "I really need a martini."

"Not yet, but Belle looks ready for her dinner," Jesse said. "While we were gone, I had the cameras rolling at all times. The steps were in the garage." Jesse got out his phone. "I checked every day and nothing was amiss."

Patrice nodded.

"Poor baby. Come on." Belle was so well trained that she never begged for food. She sat back a distance until Jane filled the bowl, stepped aside, and said "Okay," then she'd eat. "Good girl."

"You watched twenty-four hours of tape every day while we were hiding out in Panama City?" Jane asked Jesse.

"Well, there's a gadget that detects motion, so I fast-forward until I see something. And I slow it down for any motion, even if it's a gator. It doesn't take that long. Nobody comes around here. Mostly critters," Jesse said.

"So it's good we know about her," Patrice said.

"And she doesn't know we know," Jane said.

"Good catch, Patrice," Jesse said. "Now what do we do with it?"

"Can't we figure out a way to trap Abigail? As the accomplice, she'd probably turn on him."

The sky was darkening. "I've got to get those steaks on," Jesse said. "I think better when I grill."

"And while you do that, we'll have our martinis,"

Patrice said.

"You deserve to celebrate, for bringing down that scum, Tesper," Jane said.

"Also, good catch on the Abigail piece!" Jesse said.

"Well put together, Jane," Patrice agreed. "Due diligence, but I bet she's the accomplice."

Jane brought out the martinis and asked Jesse if he wanted anything.

"I'll have a beer, and save me an olive," Jesse said.

Jane knew he liked his olive soaked in vodka, but she handed him out his beer.

Such a cozy scene. She felt safe. Even if Abigail was Jesse's maid. There could be a way to work that in their favor and catch a killer, warrant or not.

Chapter Forty

Martinis in hand, Gulf in view, Jane and Patrice kicked around possible ways to catch Abigail.

"Why doesn't Jesse mention on Tuesday that his cameras are on the fritz and a tech guy will be coming out to check his system, but he can't get there until next Wednesday afternoon?" Jane said. Vodka made her think better. Up to a point.

"So she'll assume the cameras are really broken and she has to use the stairs," Patrice added. "And you'll be here. Jesse will explain your relationship and mention someone tried to kill you so you're staying with him."

"Bait." Jane drained her martini, saving an olive for Jesse. "I'll do it."

"No cameras, so she thinks the murderer, her partner, has an all-clear."

Jesse pulled the steaks off the grill, and Jane popped a vodka-soaked blue cheese olive in his mouth.

"We have a perfect plan. If we're right about Abigail and the alleged killer," Jane told Jesse.

They sat at Jesse's table, which looked like a giant piece of driftwood varnished to a high sheen, and told him their plan as they cut into their juicy steaks.

"Jane? Are you sure you want to do this?" Jesse asked.

"Sure I'm sure. There will be all your massive police backup hiding in the beach grass and the bedroom."

"You can let us figure out the tactical map, Shug."

"Good. I really want a glass of red with this awesome steak."

"Me too," said Patrice.

"You two go ahead. I'm going to skip it," Jesse said. "I have a few boxes to check on the computer." He selected a bottle of wine and opened it. Pulled two wine glasses off the shelf.

"Yes, you have tactics to figure out and a team to pull together," Patrice said.

"Don't forget someone needs to run this plan up the chain of command," Jesse said.

"I can do it after dinner," Patrice said.

Jesse gave Patrice a half glass of wine and poured more generously for Jane.

"Can you stay a few more hours?" Jesse asked Patrice.

"Yes. I'll make coffee."

"These steaks are fab, Jesse." Jane was amazed he'd already swallowed his whole.

"Thanks, Shug. I'm going to pull a team together. Map a plan. See about that warrant." He scribbled something on a sticky note and gave it to Patrice. "Chief's home number."

"I'm on it," Patrice said, finishing her last bite of steak with a swallow of red.

****

Jane did the dishes while the coffee perked.

"Jesse got anything sweet?" Patrice asked.

Jesse was in his office, which used to be a massive walk-in closet. Now it had a lock on it, and for clothes, they used an armoire Jane found in a resale shop. Jesse didn't seem to mind that she was making herself at home.

With Jane there, working at the kitchen table just was not going to happen.

Jane opened the freezer. "Ice cream. Cherry and coconut."

"No chocolate?"

"Hmmm." Jane flipped through the cabinets. "Chocolate sauce. The kind that makes a shell. My kids used to love this."

"What about cookies?"

Jane had inventoried the mostly healthy contents of Jesse's cupboards and fridge. "Not unless they're hidden."

"Scoop of each with syrup," Patrice said.

Jane made them each a double scoop and stored the rest of her steak in a container to mince for Belle while Patrice poured the coffee.

"What a place!"

"I once called it his Bat Cave."

"Ha. Where's Albert to serve our dessert?"

They giggled and sighed, and Jane's anxiety, always in the back of her mind since she was released from the hospital, vanished.

Chapter Forty-One

Saturday, Marisol called to bitch Jane out about "hitting her head." Nobody wanted to tell the kids Jane had been attacked. "Mom, I don't want to be mean, but maybe you should move to one of those retirement centers where they cook for you and things."

"I've got someone helping." An entire police force, but Marisol didn't need to know. "How's Suzy? Susan?"

Marisol let the slip pass. "She's great. Napping. We're signed up for Mommy & Me yoga."

"Will you sneak in and let me peek at her?"

Big sigh. "Let me switch to FaceTime. If she wakes up, I will never forgive you."

Soon there was Suzy in her crib, her cheeks flushed, cuddling her little stuffed fox. A gift from GG, Jane's mom. Marisol's hand swept over Suzy's silky hair. Suzy stirred, and Marisol stepped away. Suzy got smaller and smaller until Jane was face to face with Marisol in the kitchen. "Okay?"

"Yeah, thanks, honey."

"Erggg. Don't. Call. Me. That."

"Sorry. I'll let you have some free time. I know how tiring it is to be a mom," Jane said. If Marisol caught the irony, she didn't say so.

She'd call Danny Sunday. She'd be alone all weekend while the team fine-tuned their plan. Well, Jane and Patrice's plan.

With Belle on her lap, Jane watched old episodes of her favorite comedy, *Sister Issues*, and laughed. Those girls and wine were getting her through the weekend. Although it was too early for wine. She checked the cameras. Jesse had shown her how to do it through her phone. Nothing going on.

"Good time for a walk, girl?"

Belle's ears perked at the word "walk." She jumped down from her spot on Jane's lap and ran to her leash hanging by the door. Jane tucked the remote and her phone in her back pockets.

****

Jane tried to stay up for Jesse, but she didn't usually make it. Especially if she had wine. Tonight, he was really late. It was after one a.m., and she had not slept a wink. No nap. Nothing. Jane had a rule about calling Jesse while he was on duty. She didn't do it since he was just a closet office away, and he had his ringer on silent.

Her mind wandered to comparing Stan and Jesse. No comparison. Jesse was cuter, kinder, smarter, and stronger. It had become a mantra when she went into thinking about her marriage mode. Time to change her thoughts. What would it be like to live with Jesse full time? Just like this but without the killer, she imagined. They got along so well. Still, they had only been dating a few months. A month in 2019 and then two months, almost, in 2020. March and spring break were just a few days away. Three months. That wasn't enough time to know how she and Jesse would cohabitate. She gave up, sat up, disturbed Belle, who put her paw over her nose and went back to sleep. Jane tossed, then turned and still could not sleep. She groaned and left bed to swallow a sleeping pill.

The bottle said to go right to bed, and the pill would work within twenty minutes. But Jane didn't want to go to bed again. She'd been lying there for hours. She made a cup of chamomile tea and sat in the living room drinking it, looking out at what was essentially blackness. She'd had two different alcoholic drinks tonight. Not the first time, but the first time she'd followed them up with a pill. Probably not good. She looked up the combination online. "Not recommended, but everyone does it." This from a commentor in Des Moines. "I didn't drink any alcohol, but I still sleepwalked to the fridge and ate a whole cake," said anon from Ferndale. Jane wished she could throw up as she was getting more and more paranoid about what she might do under the influence of the evil sleep pill.

****

She was online binge shopping when she fell asleep. Jesse woke her up.

"Shug, why you sleeping on the sofa?"

"Huh? Oh, I was buying pans to make a cake." She looked down at her sleep shirt. "I guess I dreamed that."

"You make cake?" Jesse said.

"I used to. I used to do a lot of things."

"Let's go to bed." Jesse helped her up.

"I took a pill."

"You don't say."

"What time is it?"

"Three a.m."

"Oh, I have to sleep five more hours. Will you keep your arm around me so I don't wander into the Gulf?"

"Certainly, Shug."

Chapter Forty-Two

Jesse called Abigail, the criminal cleaner, on Monday to tell her about his supposed tech glitch. "I'm sorry, but the elevator is out of commission."

Abigail was on speaker, so Jane was ready for an outburst, but no.

"Not a problem. I'll come up by the stairs." Jane did not like the flirty voice. Abigail, with her gravel voice, did not do a great Marilyn Monroe impersonation.

"Great." At least Jesse sounded all business. "Text me when you get here, and I'll buzz you in."

"You won't be there?"

"No. Work as usual. Elevator will be fixed Thursday when you have the groceries to bring up." He didn't mention her vacuum and carry-all of cleaners.

After Jesse hung up, Jane asked him if he ordered the groceries and Abigail just brought them up, or did she do the actual shelf-to-basket herself.

Jesse gave her a funny look. "I order what I need and it's packaged for her to pick up. Why?"

Jane shrugged. "Just jealous, I guess."

Jesse smiled and blushed a little. "You're sweet, Shug. Nothing to worry about there." He caught her in a hug and then they kissed. "Okay, gotta go."

"What about telling her I'll be here?"

"I'll text her from my work phone."

Work, work, work. Jane wondered if Jesse had given

any thought to retirement. Maybe after this case was sewn up, she'd go on a real vacation. She'd always wanted to go to Greece and Rome. There was a little island where Cleopatra used to vacation with Marc Antony. The Cabo of the ancients. Temple ruins to the moon goddess. Jane loved a full moon. She'd go, with or without Jesse.

Kim called that afternoon. "What's up?"

"I think they're close," Jane said. "What's up with you?"

"Grant got fired."

"Whoa. Guess that *no guests in the pool* was just too much for Bill," Jane said.

"Indeed. Fred called to tell me they've reversed that rule and my lounge chair awaits," Kim said.

"Well deserved!"

"Guess what else?" Kim was on a roll.

"Umm. Fred got his old job back?"

"Well, yeah. But also Queenie has sold six paintings to Dennis and Rusty!"

"Oh, lawsy me! That's so excellent."

"I know. How's my baby girl?"

Jane swung the phone so Kim could see Belle sleeping on her cushion.

"Everything going okay over there?"

"Yep. I wish I could invite you, but not until the killer is locked up."

"You mean killers."

"Right."

"And that will be soon."

"Yes. They think any day now they'll have their evidence."

"Well, I'm just glad you're safe," Kim said. "Oh!

One last thing. Dennis and Rusty got married."

"No!"

"Yes!"

"They're moving to Palm Beach."

"Wow. I didn't even know he was divorced."

"Ink's not dry on the papers, but they don't like the vibe here."

"Well…"

"I know." Kim sighed. She'd never leave the Bayou. "This place attracts murderers like the jungle loves monkeys."

"I'm not leaving!" Jane said. "I think Jesse's gotten all the bad elements out of there." Jane really did think that. "But I am going on a long vacation after they get those two."

"So it's for sure partners."

"Yep."

"I'm going out to lunch with Hazel. Please tell me it's not them."

"It's not. Everything okay with her and Ethan?"

"Yep. He still tags along with Ray to poker club. Hazel says he has to force himself to lose a little bit or they get sore. Say he's counting cards."

"I never could figure out how come that's wrong."

"Superior math skills. Unfair advantage. Who knew?"

"Tell Hazel I said hi."

"Will do. You call me the minute they throw those two in the slammer, whoever they are."

"Of course. Sleepyhead is awake. Guess we'll take a walk on the beach."

Chapter Forty-Three

"What are you doing here?" Abigail said, clutching her vacuum and dropping her carry-all. Cleaning powder spilled all over the floor.

Jesse had revealed the last bit of fine-tuning of the plan to Jane before he went to work. He said he hadn't wanted to worry her. He wanted her to sleep well. He needed her reflexes sharp. Cops in combat camo were dispersed through the beach grass, inside Jesse's office closet, and parked down the street. Abigail didn't know it, but Jesse could see everything happening now on camera.

"Abigail! Hi! Jesse didn't tell you I'm staying with him?"

"I heard, but I couldn't believe it."

"Believe it. That killer went after me with a hammer, and Jesse thought I'd be safer here." Jane imagined Jesse and other team members huddled around cameras, watching and listening.

"Are you okay?" Abigail said.

"Yes. Head hard as a rock."

"I thought he was going to behead you. Something about a picture of Frida?"

That was something nobody knew. Jane's memory was foggy from that time. Maybe everyone knew. Jane asked how Abigail knew that.

"Fred told me."

"Why would Fred know?"

"Maybe he's the killer."

"Fred? He's sweet as pie. He helped us catch that first killer back in November last year," Jane said.

Abigail switched on the vacuum and proceeded to clean the ceramic floors. Jane used a steam mop after she vacuumed at home. But Abigail had no mop. Jane thought her way of cleaning was more efficient—the steamer got every grain of sand—but whatever.

Jane pretended to read the paper on her iPad. Someone from Seattle had come home from China with a contagious bug, and it was spreading into the old folks' home. She hoped Marisol and Suzy would be okay. Marisol's husband, too, of course. Jane needed to call her daughter. But she had to leave the line open for Jesse. Abigail went into the back of the house. Jane followed her.

"I washed the sheets and made the bed," Jane said.

Abigail tore off the bed clothes, including the sheets. "Are you getting paid for it?"

"No, but you don't need to do it twice."

She ignored Jane and headed for the closet.

There was a cop in the closet.

"Jesse's got his office locked up. Stuff on the investigation, you know," Jane said.

Abigail huffed.

"I brought the laundry out and put it in that basket." Jane pointed to a wicker basket full of towels. She'd never let Abigail touch her things. Or Jesse's. Again, Abigail ignored her and reached for the doorknob. Jane had turned the phone so Jesse could see what was happening, just in case the camera on the ceiling didn't catch it. Abigail's phone rang. Jane shoved her phone in her pocket.

"Abigail. I forgot to tell you," Jesse said from Jane's pocket.

Shit! Jane silenced her phone but kept it in her pocket. Luckily Abigail hadn't noticed the double voice.

"You sure did. Your girlfriend is bossing me around and not letting me do my job," Abigail said.

Jane didn't hear Jesse's reply. She was already re-making the bed.

"Yeah. Fine."

More silence.

"What about the bathroom?" Silence. "Is she moving in?" Silence. Abigail hung up.

"I could wring your neck! I need this job," she said to Jane. Jane felt a shiver pass over her entire body. Wring her neck? That wasn't happening. Jane had a gun, and Jesse had taught her how to use it. While Abigail was thrashing around with her sponge and cleaner, Jane unlocked the gun safe in the drawer on her side of the bed, strapped her shoulder harness on, and added her cozy sweater to hide it. She heard Abigail stomp into the bathroom and slam the door.

This was the part where they had to count on her to call Hammer Man. She took a long time. Jane checked her iPad to find anything else about that China flu in Seattle. Still only in the nursing home. Old and ill. Symptoms similar to flu.

Jane worried more about Suzy and her family than Hammer Man. But she was relieved. If he did come hunting for her with an ax, Jesse would be here first. The PD was recording Abigail's phone. They could hear the silences she could only guess at.

Chapter Forty-Four

Patrice and Jesse headed to Crooked Nook. They followed two cars behind their suspect, Ray. They wanted to catch Abigail before she left the house because the two of them had said nothing incriminating on their phone call. Jesse warned his team he was moving the stairs into the garage. Then he called Abigail.

"Everything okay over there?"

"Yeah. Your girlfriend's on the balcony reading a book."

"I meant the cleaning. You almost done?"

"Yes, just finishing towels since she insisted on washing the sheets and making the bed. She tidied your closet."

"That's fine."

"I suppose I'm going to have to buy a gallon of white wine along with the rest of the groceries."

"No. I'll do that. I know what she likes."

"I bet you do."

"Boyfriend job. Wine, flowers, chocolate."

Patrice almost snorted. Jesse shot her a warning look.

"How long is she going to stay?" Abigail said.

"Jane's not messy."

"No, I just—she just—puts me off my game," Abigail said.

"Stairs are still acting up. But the elevator is fixed,

so leave that way. Just call me when you need the elevator door opened."

"Now!"

Patrice wondered if the towels were dried, but she stayed silent.

"Okay, see you Thursday. Unless I work late."

"You always work late," Abigail said.

****

As she pretended to read a book on the balcony, Jane heard the stairs move in their lumbering way into the garage. She guessed she did not need her gun anymore but kept it strapped on just in case.

"What the fuck was that?" Abigail opened the slider.

"Oh, no worries. Jesse said he called you."

"He did, but *what…the…fuck*?"

"Yeah, the stairs move into the garage sometimes. But the elevator's fixed. You know these high-tech gizmos men like."

"I'm getting out of here."

Jane didn't think it was time yet. She hadn't heard the signal. No text from Patrice.

"I hear the dryer tumbling."

"You like cleaning his house so much, you do it."

Abigail didn't bother to take the vacuum with her. Or her little cleaning basket. She stuck her phone in her pocket and jammed a finger on the elevator button, which opened smoothly as usual. Jane wanted to go with her just to see the look on her face when she saw the stairs in the garage.

****

Jane, connected to Jesse through their phones, could see and hear everything going down. Bless the modern world.

Jesse's phone rang. He put it on speaker.

"Jesse, I'm in the garage." Abigail. "I thought you were opening the door. Is there a button somewhere? Like an emergency?"

"Oh, sorry. They finished fixing the elevator, but the door's going to take about two minutes. Hang tight."

Jane switched to the garage camera. Abigail found a lawn chair and sat down. She called—who else—Ray. At this point, it didn't matter what they said or did. The police would have it all cached. Jane just had to stay cozy and safe upstairs while her would-be killer walked into a trap.

Two minutes seemed like two hours, but finally the garage door opened, and Ray's car pulled into the driveway. He didn't have a knife or an ax or anything so he must be planning to execute Jane elsewhere. Ray entered the garage, then the door closed.

"Why is that closing?" Ray whipped around.

"Calm down, big boy," Abigail said.

"You're not killing anyone else, are you?" Ray asked.

"I told you. Jane needs to go. She's nosy and annoying, and she'll be my third victim, so I'll be a serial killer. I want that for myself."

Ray hung his head. "When you killed Marva, I let it go, there was positives to having her gone, so I didn't complain."

"And you didn't complain when I found alternate housing after your new wife threw me out."

"You didn't have to kill that woman. I would have given you the money to buy her house."

"Like hell you would. You said you'd give me the masterpiece that turned out to be a fake, too. All lies."

239

Ray sighed. "I don't like this."

"Too bad. You're my accomplice and that's better than being your lover ever was."

Jane video-watched Ray and Abigail as they gave up arguing about killing her. They didn't have any reason at all! Except Abigail wanted to be a serial killer. What a sick goal. Abigail was a psychopath, currently trying without success to open the elevator door so she could take a hatchet to Jane's neck. Okay, possibly Abigail was angry about the fake Frida, but how was that Jane's fault? Jane's mouth dried up, and she attempted to take a sip of water, but her hand shook so much it spilled all over the kitchen counter.

She went to the sofa and sat. If she couldn't hold a glass of water, how could she shoot a gun? It would be funny if she wasn't so scared. These people were serious about cutting her head off. Well, Abigail was, and she seemed to have Ray in some kind of thrall. Belle, sensing Jane's anxiety, jumped up on the sofa beside her and put her chin on Jane's thigh.

Jane still gripped her phone, watching her evil foes on the video screen.

Abigail paced and yelled, "Everything's messed up today. Of all days. I'll call Jesse." Abigail stabbed her phone. "What is going on?"

Jesse didn't respond. Jane knew he wanted those two right where they were. Stuck in the garage with no way out. And he wanted a confession. Which he had! Their little plan was working! She was able to sip water. Yay!

"I do not like this." Ray kicked the stairs. "Is he some kind of millionaire inventor on the side?"

"I think he's just a kid in a cop disguise. Playing

with toys." This from brainiac Abigail.

Ray looked for more things to kick, but the garage was as minimal as the house. The toolbox was locked down tight or he'd take a screwdriver to the elevator.

"Jesse texted!" Abigail said. "He knows there's a problem, and he will be here in ten minutes. I wish I could get ahold of that Jane first and finish what I started with her."

Jane held her breath. Did Jesse hear that? Did she hear that?

"Don't forget who planted the false footsteps," Ray said.

"All that means is you'll go down for murder instead of me," Abigail said.

Yes, Abigail had tried to kill her with a hammer and still wanted Jane dead. Belle had been napping, but she woke and rubbed her head against Jane's legs as if she knew Jane was upset and she wanted to comfort her. Jane pulled the dog into her arms. "My sweet little girl," she said. She hugged Belle to her heart.

"What are we going to say when he comes and I'm here?" Ray said.

"You're my boyfriend. Picking me up."

"He knows I live with Biffy."

"What? Who cares if you're my pretend boyfriend?"

"That's not it, you stupid bitch."

"Watch your mouth, asshole," Abigail said.

"Who killed Marva? You! That's who. I bailed you out then because I wanted the penthouse and it seemed easy enough. But then you had to kill Loni and left her dead in the bushes just so you could crash in her house! You're a cold-blooded bitch, and I ought to turn you in."

Ray's words made Jane pat her gun. These were

very bad people. What if they started shooting up the ceiling, Jane's floor? *Jesse, get here now*, she thought.

Jane watched as Abigail stared Ray down.

"You didn't tell me the painting was fake," Ray said.

"I didn't know it was fake. Nobody knew," Abigail said.

Ray was still pacing. "Except Jane. And Queenie. And Jane's neighbor who found it in your 'perfect' hiding spot. Ha."

"Shaddup and let me think!" Abigail said.

Listening in to these two was shocking. Ray was not the killer at all. And Grant had not been Hammer Man. It had been Abigail's gravel voice behind that face mask, not a man's.

Well, she'd gotten a few things wrong. Of course it would be a woman who'd think of something like the angel wings. Of course a woman would remember that an art expert sometimes helped the police. And she'd used that angle to take them down all the wrong roads.

Had the police figured this out? Jesse had told Jane Ray was the murder suspect. Was he just hearing the real story now? She could use a drink, but with the way things were going, she might need her gun yet. Guns and wine did not go together.

"Where's that motherfucker?" Ray said.

"He'll be here in five minutes."

Jane felt like she was watching a true crime show on television. The focus was not great, but the story was very good. Except she was the one they were after. Belle whimpered. They got up, and Jane fed her. Jesse better be here soon, or Belle would have her first accident. Jane was so mad at Abigail. *What a psycho. She could have killed me. I could have brain damage.*

Jane realized the second victim had lived close to the bayou where it curved away from the condos and into Lake Seminole. Maybe she'd seen something. Maybe, as Ray believed, the killing had been opportunistic. It had to be Ray who hauled Marva's body down to the bayou. Abigail wasn't physically able. But why kill poor Loni?

"Now I'll never get a chance to kill that nosy bitch." Jane jumped when Abigail spoke.

"You have to stop killing people! I don't like it," Ray said.

"You know you do."

"Well, I liked helping with Marva, but that's it. They're calling us serial killers, and it's not true. I'm not in on any more killings. Not even to cover up for you."

Ray pulled a shovel off the wall and banged Abigail hard on the head just as the garage door opened. The garage filled with cops in sand camo. Jesse fitted cuffs on Ray while Patrice cuffed a dazed Abigail and read them their rights. Jane stayed upstairs, glued to Jesse's remote system that played out what was happening in the garage. Ray and Abigail were secured, and their images walked out of the camera frame. Jane ran out to the balcony and, leaning over the side, saw them placed in the back seat of a labeled cop car, not Jesse's plain detective car.

Patrice left. Jesse stayed and took Jane's statement from the house.

Chapter Forty-Five

"Good thing we caught that confession on tape," Jesse said, hugging Jane. "I have a little work to do downtown before I come back home for the night. Will you be okay?"

"Yeah, sure. As long as Hammer Woman is behind bars."

"Didn't see that coming! But yes, she's probably already in a cell. Two murders and assault with intent to kill." Jesse finally stopped squeezing her and left to finish his job locking up bad people.

Jane waited until the last police car left, then she took Belle out for a tinkle. She kept her gun on because you never knew.

After a walk on the white sand beach, Jane and Belle went back to Jesse's place and Jane took off her sweater, locked up her gun, and slipped out of the shoulder holster. It was an uncomfortable thing, but Jesse had warned her not to stick a Glock down the back of her jeans like they did in the movies.

Where had she put those pills?

Jane had done everything she could to stop her hands shaking, but they wouldn't stop. The pill would help. She took it and while Belle slept on her cushion, she opened the balcony door. It was a coolish day even though spring was right around the corner. She wore one of Jesse's sweatshirts, of which he had an abundance.

Jane laughed, but in truth she was worried about Marisol. Seattle had a few more cases of that flu from China. Old people flu, they were calling it.

Jane pulled her phone from her pants pocket and dialed Marisol, who took her time answering.

"Hello, Mom. I'm not dead yet."

"That's not funny."

"Well, then. No earthquake yet."

Jane did tend to worry about everything from strange viruses to earthquakes to global warming when it came to her family in Seattle. Which was on a major fault line. But she didn't say that to Marisol.

Jane told Marisol about Ray and Abigail. Just that they'd been arrested.

"Good!" Marisol said. "Mom, can you stay out of trouble?"

"I think so." They both laughed.

"Cop boyfriend, trouble's going to follow you."

"This is a pretty quiet town compared to Detroit."

"Seattle has it's crime spots," Marisol said.

"I know. So here is better than most places," Jane said.

"You just happened to get there during a bad spell." Marisol was being kind. As her gran liked to say, "Will wonders never cease."

"Good time with Granny and Pops?" Jane asked.

"Yes. Especially Suzy." Marisol switched to video phone. "Let me see your little Tinkerbell."

Jane flipped the phone to Belle. "Say hi, Belle."

"Arf," Belle said straight to the phone.

"She's sure cute. And those waves look nice."

"Come anytime!"

"To Jesse's house?"

245

Jane forgot she was not home at the Bayou.

"Wherever. Jesse's place is small, but I'll be moving home any day now, just down the road a piece."

"You're talking like a southern gal." Marisol was finally talking like a nice daughter.

"Or," Jane said, "I could stay here with Jesse and you and your family could stay at my place. We're only…"

"I know. Down the road a piece."

They laughed again.

"I'm glad you're okay, Mom. Suzy's sleeping or she'd say so too."

"I notice you're all calling her Suzy."

"Your fault!" Marisol said, but the laugh was still in her voice. "Did you call Granny yet?"

"Nope, you're my first call."

"Better call her."

"Yeah, I'd better, after I text Danny. It'll be on the local news by now. Love you, sweetie."

"Suzy is one thing, but please don't call me sweetie."

"I thought you hated your name?" Jane said. The first "Marisol" was a mostly forgotten artist who became attached to Pop Art when she hung out with Andy Warhol. Jane had done her dissertation on her. And named her beloved child after her.

"I got used to it. Fits with Seattle. Say hi to Gran. Love you too."

Jane texted Danny, then called her mother who had heard the entire report on the local news but was okay because she knew Jesse would keep Jane safe and St. Pete could sleep tight again tonight.

Jesse came home after dark, and they sat inside

facing the Gulf. It was storming, and the palm trees streamed out in the air. Still beautiful. They were drinking hot tea and honey because Jane had talked to so many people on the phone her voice was scratchy.

"Stay one more night, Shug," Jesse said.

"Happy to," she said and kissed his cheek. "You need to tell me why Abigail killed the poor lady on Orange Blossom."

Jesse was silent.

"They just said the what on the news, not the why. Why'd she do it? Was it really just for a place to sleep?" Jane couldn't figure it out.

"You might not like what you hear," Jesse said.

Jane couldn't imagine. "I can take it. What's going to drive me mad is not knowing. Especially if it's something to do with me, which I cannot see how it could."

"Well, it's not your fault. Not even a little bit," Jesse said.

"I know that." Jane didn't know it.

"Okay then. Abigail heard about the trolley accident."

Jane tried to think. "Abigail was not there when I told that story."

"She'd been researching Frida. We found that on her laptop. And we found the Frida diary and another book of Frida self-portraits at Loni's along with clothing belonging to Abigail."

"Loni. Murder victim two."

"Yes. Abigail was living there."

"And planning more killings, sounds like."

Jane sighed. What had happened to Frida was tragic. Abigail had used an artist to terrorize a town known for its devotion to artists. Then Jane felt anger creeping into her heart. She knew the murder on Orange Blossom was not her fault.

"I'm sad and mad at the same time, but I don't blame myself. I wasn't gossiping or telling that story about Frida's accident to be spiteful. It's the explanation for the *Broken Column* self-portrait. That's all. For Frida, it meant a life of pain and suffering."

"But to a psychopath, to Abigail, the story triggered blood lust. Not to mention she was convinced the woman, Loni, had seen her and Ray with Marva dead in a wheelbarrow."

"Is that even possible?"

"No, but Abigail had convinced herself it was," Jesse said.

Jane knew all about psychopaths and sociopaths. There were more in the world than people realized. She nodded. "Abigail also got off on the idea of pain. She liked inflicting it. Just regular pain, like the way she tormented Ray in the garage."

"Also, Abigail was angry that the painting was a fake. She thought she was going to be rich, or at least have a home, and that was taken away from her. And she'd have Ray, which didn't happen either. That made her temper even hotter," Jesse said.

"So when I walked by Loni's house, I noticed a For Sale sign. Did she pretend to be a buyer? Or a Realtor? How else would she get into her house?"

"Yes, we think that's what happened. Abigail made up a story, so Loni let her in. The night before your walk. She shoved her into the landscaping next to the house after dark. She got the pole from a stack in the garage. Loni had been getting some work done on her ancient plumbing. You just happened to be the first person to walk by with a trained police dog."

"So Ray had nothing to do with the second murder?"

"Nothing more than we have on tape. Someone cleaned up, but they didn't get everything. We got a good print from Abigail on the pipe. That's how we can prove beyond a doubt it was her."

Chapter Forty-Six

Jane and Jesse had a dinner break and were in bed, still discussing the case.

"So far, Abigail's psych eval has been inconclusive, but it's easy to see, once you know how ruthlessly she plotted, that she has to be cold-blooded," Jesse said.

"Women don't kill that often. And not like that."

"More in self-defense, more in subtle ways like poison. They don't plan elaborate scenes like Abigail did," Jesse agreed.

"So, she's likely psychotic."

"We think so. A professional in that area is questioning Abigail now."

Jane didn't say anything about it, but Jesse's voice was fading fast.

"You should get some rest," she said.

"I won't argue with that," he said.

****

The next morning Patrice stopped by with a coffee cake and some news.

"Jesse's sleeping," Jane said.

"So not just faking to get out of work?" Patrice said.

"Ha-ha. You know Jesse. Such a slacker." Jane lowered her voice. "But really, he's feeling like shit. It happened quick. One minute he was okay, just tired. He closed his eyes, then he woke up for a minute and asked for water. Said he had a raging sore throat. You don't want to get around his germs."

They took their coffee cake and fresh mugs of coffee out on the balcony. Jane closed the door quietly.

"He'll be sorry he missed this newsflash, but you can tell it. And it will be on the news in an hour, I bet. They'll probably interrupt regular programming."

"That good?" Jane asked. "Do tell!"

"Okay. Ray spilled the beans on Abigail but good. He showed remorse, if not for Marva's death, then at least for Loni Andresson's. He didn't want to chop your head off. He'll get a lighter sentence. One accessory to murder instead of two first degree murders, which is what Abigail is getting." Patrice took a huge bite of her coffee cake and chewed it with a satisfied air.

Jane looked again. Patrice was also tired. Her eyes were drooping as she slurped coffee.

"Were you up all night?"

Patrice nodded and took another bite of her cake. "Sugar and caffeine will perk me up."

"At least for a little while," Jane said.

"I admit, I had to brag to Jesse. But you'll do," Patrice said.

"Oh gee. I'm honored."

"You know how Abigail was 'going out' with Ray. Even when Marva was alive?" Patrice said.

"Yes. That's not still a secret?"

"No. But it was a secret that Abigail nailed Grant."

"Nailed as in…"

"Had intercourse with. Yes," Patrice said.

"Another married man."

"A married man who wanted the penthouse."

"She has no morals when it comes to sex, or when murder is the sin. She had her keys to the penthouse and

251

one night on Marva's regular book-club meeting, she talked Ray into going up there to steal the Kahlo. Ray was easing it off the wall when Marva, who had not gone to book club, woke from a wine nap and heard Abigail, who wasn't trying to be quiet. Ray and Marva got into a shouting match, and Marva never saw Abigail coming with the bowl." Patrice stopped to glug the rest of her coffee.

"Her modus operandi—head bashing!" Jane said, reflexively rubbing her skull. She wished the patch of hair the surgeon shaved off would grow back. It was about two inches now and stuck out like a sassy tongue. From the side of her head.

"Abigail took the painting and grabbed the angel wings. Ray helped her move the body. Then he planted the false footprints. Abigail had leverage against him. And it worked.

"Ray, up to this point, was only guilty of knowing some things and helping with a cover-up of his wife's murder. He knew he had the penthouse back. He would not have to split assets with Marva. And he had nothing to do with the actual murder."

"Problem for Abigail."

"She lied to him and told him she hadn't known it was fake. But she did know because the two of you had that conversation after the happy hour at the pool."

"Right. I forgot about that."

"Devil's in the details," Patrice said.

Chapter Forty-Seven

Jesse recovered from his flu, at least they hoped it was flu, but he did not want Jane to leave. And she did not want to go.

"What's going to happen to us?" Jane said. "We moved in together by mistake."

Jesse laughed. "I like it. Don't you?"

"I like your regular hours," Jane said. She looked out the slider at the Gulf, calm today. It reminded her of an old movie about the end of the world. People waiting for nuclear fallout to hit their beach. They were drinking, just like she and Jesse were. But they knew it was coming. Jane shivered. Set down her glass of wine and moved into Jesse's arms.

He held her. "Shug, I love you. I love having you here. I want you to stay. I know it's short notice, but your choice, a ring or a promise."

Jane looked at the empty water. The empty beach. The house was small, but it had plenty of life. Belle and Jesse were great companions.

"We could just be engaged. Not married. Maybe go back and forth to Winding Bayou for a while. At least until we've been together a year," Jane said.

"Thanksgiving will be a year. But let's spend every night together at one place or the other," Jesse said.

"Yes. And Christmas weddings are nice. As long as my family can all be here in St. Pete," Jane said.

Belle brought over a stuffed dinosaur and dropped it at Jesse's feet.

"Belle approves," Jane said.

"I've been thinking. I bet you like pink diamonds," Jesse said.

"I do," Jane said. "Emerald cut. Rose gold ring."

"That's settled then."

They sealed the deal with a satisfyingly long kiss, a kiss that flamed hot down Jane's throat. Wait. Didn't Jesse have a burning sore throat when he got sick?

"Um…" Jane broke off the kiss.

"What's wrong, Shug?"

"You're burning me up," Jane said. "I need a drink of water." She crossed her fingers behind her back.

A word about the author...

Cynthia Harrison has written eight books with The Wild Rose Press. She recently moved to Florida's Gulf Coast where her current series is set. She's working on her next novel.

Thank you for purchasing
this publication of The Wild Rose Press, Inc.

For questions or more information
contact us at
info@thewildrosepress.com.

The Wild Rose Press, Inc.
www.thewildrosepress.com